SUPERTOYS LAST ALL SUMMER LONG

SUPERTOYS LAST ALL SUMMER LONG

and
Other Stories of Future Time

Brian Aldiss

St. Martin's Griffin 🦜 New York

"Attempting to Please," some elements published in the *Guardian* 16 July 1999. "Supertoys Last All Summer Long," first published in *Harper's Bazaar,* December 1969. "Apogee Again," written for the birthday of Michael Moorcock. "Headless," first published in the *Daily Telegraph,* 23 April 1994. "Nothing in Life is Ever Enough," first published in Paris, June 1999 as "Rien dans La Vie N'est Jamais Suffisant." "Pause Button," broadcast on Channel Four, 1997. Steppenpferd," first published in the *Magazine of Fantasy and Science Fiction,* February 2000. "Cognitive Ability and the Light Bulb," first published in *Nature,* 20 January 2000. "Dark Society," first published in *Dante's Disciples,* Editor, Peter Crowther, 1995. "Becoming the Full Butterfly," first published in *The Secret of This Book,* Brian Aldiss, 1995. "A Whiter Mars," first performed at the Conference of the Fantastic, Fort Lauderdale, Florida, March 1995.

All other items here published for the first time.

www.stmartins.com

ISBN 0-312-28061-0

First published in Great Britain by Orbit

10 9 8 7 6 5 4 3 2

CONTENTS

Foreword: Attempting to Please

'**S**upertoys Last All Summer Long' is the story of a young boy who, whatever he does, cannot please his mother. He is puzzled about this, not realising that he is an android, a cunning construct of artificial intelligence, as is his one ally, his teddy bear.

This was the story that greatly affected Stanley Kubrick and he was keen to make it into a movie. After some persuasion, I sold him the film rights. For some while, I worked on a possible screenplay with him.

Hardly surprisingly, I found him genial but exacting. After all, his independence was hard-won. Stanley drove himself just as hard as he drove everyone else.

I saw an example of this independence when the top brass of Warner Brothers wished to meet Kubrick. Pleading a hatred of flying, Kubrick got the directors, on whose financial support he relied, to come over to London. Once there, they invited him down to town to meet them at their hotel. Kubrick said he was too busy. So the Warner Brothers executives made a further trip to St Albans to meet him.

The treatment of his staff was stamped by the same self-regard: genial but exacting. He needed not only to sustain his independence but to nourish his myth, the myth of a creative but eccentric hermit-genius.

My relationship with Stanley was a friendly one. I mentioned his three science fiction films in my history of science fiction, *Billion Year Spree*, remarking that *Dr Strangelove*, *2001: A Space Odyssey* and *Clockwork Orange* made him 'the great SF writer of the age'. Kubrick happened to buy the book and was pleased by the remark.

He phoned me one day in the mid-seventies. It was a bit of a surprise. He entered into a long monologue, presumably to test out my listening powers. Whatever it was, I must have passed the test, because he invited me to lunch with him. We met in July 1976, at a restaurant in Boreham Wood.

At that time Stanley resembled Che Guevara, complete with boots, jungle greens, beret crammed over curly hair, and beard. We talked movies, SF, and drink. It was a thoroughly enjoyable conversation, long protracted.

Stanley's *Barry Lyndon* had been released in the previous year and although the photography is of unparalleled beauty, its perfect cut-glass frigidity had proved not to be to popular taste. Perhaps Kubrick was uncertain what to film next. Our relationship was cordial; we met for one or two lunches over the years, and always discussed what sort of film would be successful.

I recommended *Martian Time-Slip*, a sixties novel by Philip K. Dick. Stanley was not interested. Later, two years of my life were to be occupied by trying to get this novel on to the screen, co-writing the screenplay with my then media agent, Frank Hatherley.

My wife Margaret and I drove over to Castle Kubrick a

couple of times and lunched with Stanley and his artist wife, Christiane, whose bright canvases lit many a wall. Stanley liked and admired actors. He thought Peter Sellars a genius. He had a casual repertory he trusted, such as Sterling Hayden, Philip Stone, Norman Rossiter and Sellers. 'You don't need this bit of dialogue,' he said on one occasion. 'Throw it out. A good actor can convey all that just with a look.'

While filming Stephen King's novel, *The Shining*, he was necessarily elusive. He surfaced again in August 1982, referring in a letter to our previous lunch when 'we spent most of the time talking about *Star Wars* and why fairly dumb stories might really be an art form'. We had certainly had an absorbing discussion, trying to enumerate the elements that would make a successful fairy-tale-like SF film. These elements included a lad of humble origins who must fight a monstrous evil, a group of assorted chums, various challenges overcome, the evil defeated against all odds and the youth winning the hand of a princess. Then we laughed: we had described *Star Wars* almost blow for blow.

That letter from Stanley continued with talk of my story, *Supertoys*. At Stanley's request, I had sent him some of my books, including *The Malacia Tapestry* and *Moment of Eclipse*, a collection of my short stories published by Faber and Faber, which contains 'Supertoys Last All Summer Long'. Stanley wrote, 'What has remained with me, however, is the persistent belief that the short story is a fine beginning for a longer story, though, sadly, I have had no further ideas about how it could be developed. Anyway, I begin to think the old subconscious doesn't really begin to work on something which it doesn't own . . .'

This story – a vignette, really – was first published in *Harper's Bazaar* in December 1969; in 1982, I had to deal with major income tax problems, so I reluctantly sold it to Kubrick. He bought most of the rights to it; I recall that the phrase 'in perpetuity' occurred in the contract rather frequently. With hindsight, one sees that owning the story made no great difference to Stanley's creative processes. He still could not make a movie out of it.

After much toing and froing among agents, the contract was signed in November 1982. So I went to work with him on the screenplay.

Every day, a limo would come to my door on Boars Hill, and I would be driven to Castle Kubrick, Stanley's Blenheim-sized pad outside St Albans. Stanley had often been up half the night, wandering his great desolate rooms choked with apparatus. He would materialise in a rumpled way saying, 'Let's have some fresh air, Brian.'

We would open a door on to his rolling acres. Stanley would light up a cigarette and we would stroll forward, half the distance of a cricket pitch, with Stanley puffing away. 'That's enough fresh air,' he would say. Back in we would go for the day. It was a kind of joke. Our relationship was also kind of joking.

At one point, after bringing a new character into the script, Stanley asked, 'Brian, what do people do who don't make films or write science fiction?' He was so intelligent, so dedicated to his craft. Unfortunately he was also impatient and did not permit argument or the consideration of any line of development he did not immediately like.

Initially, I could not visualise how this vignette might be developed into a full-scale movie. Then, one morning at breakfast, I suddenly saw it. 'I've got it!' I told Margaret. I phoned Stanley. 'Come on over,' he said.

I went. I told him. He didn't like it.

And there the matter was closed. He would never half accept anything, turn it around, see if there was not some merit in it. While this was the sign of a clear-sighted man, perhaps there was also a weakness in the approach.

Rather ominously, when I first went to work with him, Stanley gave me a beautifully illustrated copy of the story of Pinocchio. I could not or would not see the parallels between David, my five-year-old android, and the wooden creature who becomes human. It emerged that Stanley wished David to become human, and wished, also, to have the Blue Fairy materialise. Never consciously rewrite old fairy stories, I'd say.

To work with Stanley was certainly instructive. My trouble was that I had enjoyed my independence for some thirty years; I did not relish working with, and certainly not *under*, anyone else. But our relationship was amiable. If we were stuck, we would take a stroll and go to say hello to Christiane. She was usually painting in a large empty room, with magnificent windows looking out across the Kubrickian veldt. Stanley also liked to cook our lunch, which generally consisted of steak and string beans.

I had refused to see my vignette as a full-scale motion picture. Stanley reassured me. He said that it was easier to enlarge a short story than to shrink a novel into a film. A film contained at most sixty scenes, whereas a novel might contain hundreds, one fading into another at no extra expense.

Besides, he said, he had taken Arthur C. Clarke's short story, 'The Sentinel', like 'Supertoys' two thousand words long, and made it into a major picture. We could do the same with my story. Only later did I see the flaw in this line of reasoning: while Arthur's story looks outwards to the solar system, my story looks inwards.

We got down to serious work. Every day, I noted our progress in a large red book. When I returned home that evening, Margaret and I would have a chat about things over a drink. Then came supper, after which I would go to the study and write up the notes in screenplay form without dialogue, as Stanley insisted. These passages were then faxed to Stanley. At that time, it was still smart to have a fax machine; we could not have worked so easily without it.

That task completed, I would write up in a private diary the events and non-events of the day. There was for instance the week when it seemed as if the world was sliding into recession. Stanley kept a close eye on the money markets. He came into the room where I was working and advised, gloomily, 'Brian, I should sell all your stocks and shares and buy gold bars.' My one gold bar would have been the size of a bar of Wrigley's chewing gum.

Next day, when we sat down together, he might well take up the previous day's work only to dismiss it completely. No wonder we smoked heavily and drank gallons of coffee . . .

But for a while all went well. I wrote a linking episode called *Taken Out* in February 1983 and faxed it to him overnight. He rang me, full of enthusiasm. 'It's just brilliant. I'm so thrilled. The way to do SF must be to tell it as if it's just ordinary, with nothing that needs to be explained.'

Me: 'In other words, you treat the reader/viewer as if he also is part of the future world you're describing.'

Stanley: 'I guess so, you just don't go into all the gory scientific details.'

Me: 'The more you explain, the less convincing it gets.'

Stanley: 'You seem to have two modes of writing – brilliant and not so damned good.'

We had our stand-offs. I never again pleased him as well as with *Taken Out*. Though we often rocked with laughter while working, we made no progress. Plot line after plot line tunnelled into the sands.

Stanley would have nothing of my reliance on narrative. Pointing out that while a movie can contain at most sixty scenes, he claimed that it needed only about eight 'non-submersible units', as he called them (we got to three before we broke up, by adapting two of my early stories, 'All the World's Tears' and 'Blighted Profile' to the line of the original short story).

This method of non-submersible units shows in *2001*. Part of the mystery of the film derives from contrasts between its disparate sections. The method works at its best in *The Shining*. Here, blackboards announcing starkly 'A Month Later' or, simply, 'Tuesday 4 p.m.' warn the audience pleasurably that something awful is going to happen and that Jack Nicholson is going to be a little more over the top than before.

Stanley was a secretive man. He never discussed what else he was working on. So far the most perceptive book on Kubrick's work is Thomas Allen Nelson's *Kubrick: Inside a Film Artist's Maze* (Indiana University Press, 1982). Nelson makes largely convincing claims for what others may see as mere inconsistencies within *The Shining* (1980), explaining them as givens in any horror fantasy. Still, the film could have been improved if some shading had been given to the character of Wendy Torrance (played by Shelley Duvall). Methinks the lady doth gibber too much.

It was surprising to discover that Stanley was uncertain where to go next. He asked me once what sort of movie he could make that would gross as much as *Star Wars*, while enabling him still to retain his reputation for having a social conscience.

When I arrived at Castle Kubrick on one occasion, he would talk only about Spielberg's *E.T.* Perhaps he admired the way much of *E.T.* is filmed from hip height, in emulation of a child's vision, as some of *The Shining* is shot by Steadicam from young Danny Torrance's viewpoint. He loved science fiction movies. We sat through most of Ridley Scott's *Blade Runner* on laser disc.

Stanley was convinced that one day artificial intelligence would take over and mankind would be superseded. Humans were not reliable enough, not intelligent enough. During one of our frequent impasses, we discussed the possibility of the Soviet Union collapsing and the West sending in robot tanks and androids to save what could be saved. It was a dramatic enough event to excite our imaginations. This was in 1982 and we understood there might be economic collapse in the USSR – but how would it come about? What would the circumstances be?

After a day or two, we retreated from the idea. But let us suppose we had thought events through, and had been able exactly to replicate the true events of 1989, only seven years in the future. Suppose we had created a Gorbachev figure as president of the Soviet Union, had shown Hungary opening its gates for East Germans to pour into Berlin and the West, had shown the Berlin Wall being breached, Communist governments voting themselves out of power, dictators executed, the end of the Cold War declared and the biggest movement ever in one day of the

European peoples. In fact, an unique moment in world history.

And if we had put all this on the screen in 1982? No one would have believed it. Even SF is the art of the plausible. So, critics might say, there lies SF's weakness. It is real life which takes on the art of the incredible, as it did at the end of the nineteen-eighties – and continues still to do with the rise and expansion of the European Union.

The years dragged by. We were getting nowhere. Stanley became more impatient. Still the Blue Fairy rose from the dead. I had the feeling I was being swallowed up, while trying to remain a husband and father.

Stanley perceived a key problem with David, the android boy. David could be presented on film by faking. But Stanley's perfectionism suggested that a real android might be built. We went into that possibility in some depth. The first technological hurdle to be overcome was to make the little chap move in a manner resembling a real boy – to walk and turn and sit, etc. Film technology has progressed since then, of course, and nowadays, computer simulation would do the job.

In 1987, *Full Metal Jacket* was released. This late take on the Vietnam War became a hit in Japan, while proving less successful elsewhere. With the aid of thirty-six palm trees imported from Spain, Kubrick created Vietnam within the ruins of a site in London's East End (prior to the building of Canary Wharf). 'It's almost impossible to construct plausible ruins,' Stanley claimed, 'and winter sunsets in England resemble sunsets in Vietnam.' The actors in bare buff were filmed in winter cold, with blower heaters just off-camera to keep the gooseflesh from showing. Ah, the magic of the movies!

By 1990, we were in difficulties. Agents and lawyers

were exchanging letters. Stanley and I were working on the idea of flooding New York, only to have the Blue Fairy emerge from the depths. I tried to persuade Stanley that he should create a great modern myth to rival *Dr Strangelove* and *2001*, and to avoid fairy tale.

It was absurd of me. I was wheeled out of the picture.

He never said goodbye or uttered a word of unmeant thanks. Instead, another cigarette was lit, the back was turned. And 'Supertoys' was rechristened 'AI' – and destined never to be made by him.

Stanley was two kinds of genius. Besides his films, with their compelling variety, he had the gift of keeping the world from his creative door, and cultivating his legend as a hermit. He always knew time was short.

Geniuses do not bother with ordinary courtesies. They have other things on their mind. You do well not to resent their meaner habits. And even Arthur C. Clarke, Stanley's partner on *2001*, could not expand my vignette into a major movie. There's a lesson there for all of us, if only I could think what it was.

It was a relief to go my own sweet way again. For a few years, I had served as one of Kubrick's tentacles. He had many tentacles. On one occasion, as we were struggling with the concept of using a real android, Stanley claimed that Americans saw robots only as menaces. It was the Japanese who really liked robots; so they would breed the electronic wizards most likely to construct the first genuine androids. He summoned Tony Frewin, his faithful right-hand man.

'Get me Mitsubishi on the line.' (Let's just say it was Mitsubishi, since I have forgotten which company it actually was.)

'Who do you want to speak to at Mitsubishi, Stanley?'

'Get Mr Mitsubishi on the line.'

A while later, the phone rang. Stanley picked it up. A voice at the other end said, 'Oh, Mr Stanley Kubrick? Is Mr Mitsubishi speaking. How can I help you?'

Everyone on the planet knew the name of Stanley Kubrick. One must expect such a man to be unlike the likes of us.

So why was 'Supertoys' not filmed? The people who followed me, each trying without success to work the trick, were forced to travel along the lines that Stanley Kubrick had laid down.

My belief is that he was basically mistaken. Obsessed with the big blockbuster SF movies of the time, he was determined to take my sorrowing domestic scene out into the galaxy. After all, he had wrought similarly to great success with Clarke's story.

But 'The Sentinel' looks outwards to begin with. It speaks of a mystery elsewhere, whereas 'Supertoys' speaks of a mystery within. David suffers because he does not know he is a machine. Here is the real drama; as Mary Shelley said of her *Frankenstein*, it 'speaks to the mysterious fears of our nature'.

A possible film could be made of 'Supertoys' showing David facing his real nature. It comes as a shock to realise he is a machine. He malfunctions. Perhaps his father takes him to a factory where a thousand identical androids step off the line. Does he autodestruct? The audience should be subjected to a tense and alarming drama of claustrophobia, to be left with the final questions, 'Does it matter that David is a machine? Should it matter? And to what extent are we all machines?'

Behind such metaphysical puzzles remains the simple story – the story that attracted Stanley Kubrick – of a boy who was never able to please his mother. A story of love rejected.

Stanley Kubrick died in 1999. The mystery man was news. I grew tired of giving filmed interviews. I had a novel I was trying to write. It occurred to me to re-read my 'Supertoys' story. And then I found I was telling myself what happened next. Thirty years after that first instalment, I wrote a second story, continuing the adventures of David and Teddy.

A visitor called. A very congenial visitor, Jan Harlan, Stanley's brother-in-law and business associate. Jan wanted me to appear in a documentary he was making about Kubrick's life. At the end of the afternoon, I gave him the new story, 'Supertoys When Winter Comes'.

Jan sent the story to Steven Spielberg, who has inherited Stanley's unfinished works.

Meanwhile, I had written to Spielberg. In my letter, I suggested that David might meet with a thousand replicas of himself. Spielberg liked the idea and Jan offered to buy the sentence containing the idea. Of course, one is charmed and amused by the idea of selling off a sentence, one sentence. But by then I had seen how the David cycle should end, and had written a third story. The three stories between them contain in outline all that is needful for my idea of a motion picture. No flooded New York, no Blue Fairy. Just an intense and powerful drama of love and intelligence.

The story, 'Supertoys in Other Seasons', was sent by Jan to Spielberg. It includes that magic sentence.

By an amicable arrangement with Warner Brothers, Spielberg has now acquired all three Supertoy stories.

While I am happy to be the only man who has sold stories to two magnificent film-makers, Kubrick and

Spielberg, I understand that Spielberg has agreed to film 'Supertoys' – now entitled *AI* – as Kubrick was planning to do.

Production began on Long Island in June 2000. The movie will be released, appropriately enough, in 2001.

Supertoys Last All Summer Long

In Mrs Swinton's garden, it was always summer. The lovely almond trees stood about it in perpetual leaf. Monica Swinton plucked a saffron-coloured rose and showed it to David.

'Isn't it lovely?' she said.

David looked up at her and grinned without replying. Seizing the flower, he ran with it across the lawn and disappeared behind the kennel where the mowervator crouched, ready to cut or sweep or roll when the moment dictated. She stood alone on her impeccable plastic gravel path.

She had tried to love him.

When she made up her mind to follow the boy, she found him in the courtyard floating the rose in his paddling pool. He stood in the pool engrossed, still wearing his sandals.

'David, darling, do you have to be so awful? Come in at once and change your shoes and socks.'

He went with her without protest, his dark head bobbing at the level of her waist. At the age of five, he showed no fear of the ultra-sonic dryer in the kitchen. But before his mother could reach for a pair of slippers, he wriggled away and was gone into the silence of the house.

He would probably be looking for Teddy.

Monica Swinton, twenty-nine, of graceful shape and lambent eye, went and sat in her living-room arranging her limbs with taste. She began by sitting and thinking; soon she was just sitting. Time waited on her shoulder with the manic sloth it reserves for children, the insane and wives whose husbands are away improving the world. Almost by reflex, she reached out and changed the wavelength of her windows. The garden faded; in its place, the city centre rose by her left hand, full of crowding people, blow-boats, and buildings – but she kept the sound down. She remained alone. An overcrowded world is the ideal place in which to be lonely.

The directors of Synthank were eating an enormous luncheon to celebrate the launching of their new product. Some of them wore plastic face-masks popular at the time. All were elegantly slender, despite the rich food and drink they were putting away. Their wives were elegantly slender, despite the food and drink they too were putting away. An earlier and less sophisticated generation would have regarded them as beautiful people, apart from their eyes. Their eyes were hard and calculating.

Henry Swinton, Managing Director of Synthank, was about to make a speech.

'I'm sorry your wife couldn't be with us to hear you,' his neighbour said.

'Monica prefers to stay at home thinking beautiful thoughts,' said Swinton, maintaining a smile.

'One would expect such a beautiful woman to have beautiful thoughts,' said the neighbour.

Take your mind off my wife, you bastard, thought Swinton, still smiling.

He rose to make his speech amid applause.

After a couple of jokes, he said, 'Today marks a real breakthrough for the company. It is now almost ten years since we put our first synthetic life-forms on the world market. You all know what a success they have been, particularly the miniature dinosaurs. But none of them had intelligence.

'It seems like a paradox that in this day and age we can create life but not intelligence. Our first selling line, the Crosswell Tape, sells best of all, and is the most stupid of all.'

Everyone laughed.

'Though three-quarters of our overcrowded world is starving, we are lucky here to have more than enough, thanks to population control. Obesity's our problem, not malnutrition. I guess there's nobody round this table who doesn't have a Crosswell working for him in the small intestine, a perfectly safe parasite tape-worm that enables its host to eat up to fifty per cent more food and still keep his or her figure. Right?'

General nods of agreement.

'Our miniature dinosaurs are almost equally stupid. Today, we launch an intelligent synthetic life-form – a full-size serving-man.

'Not only does he have intelligence, he has a controlled amount of intelligence. We believe people would be afraid of a being with a human brain. Our serving-man has a small computer in his cranium.

'There have been mechanicals on the market with mini-computers for brains – plastic things without life,

3

supertoys – but we have at last found a way to link computer circuitry with synthetic flesh.'

David sat by the long window of his nursery, wrestling with paper and pencil. Finally, he stopped writing and began to roll the pencil up and down the slope of the desk-lid.

'Teddy!' he said.

Teddy lay on the bed against the wall, under a book with moving pictures and a giant plastic soldier. The speech-pattern of his master's voice activated him and he sat up.

'Teddy, I can't think what to say!'

Climbing off the bed, the bear walked stiffly over to cling to the boy's leg. David lifted him and set him on the desk.

'What have you said so far?'

'I've said –' He picked up his letter and stared hard at it. 'I've said, "Dear Mummy, I hope you're well just now. I love you."'

There was a long silence, until the bear said, 'That sounds fine. Go downstairs and give it to her.'

Another long silence.

'It isn't quite right. She won't understand.'

Inside the bear, a small computer worked through its program of possibilities. 'Why not do it again in crayon?'

David was staring out of the window. 'Teddy, you know what I was thinking? How do you tell what are real things from what aren't real things?'

The bear shuffled its alternatives. 'Real things are good.'

'I wonder if time is good. I don't think Mummy likes time very much. The other day, lots of days ago, she said that time went by her. Is time real, Teddy?'

'Clocks tell the time. Clocks are real. Mummy has clocks so she must like them. She has a clock on her wrist next to her dial.'

David had started to draw an airliner on the back of his letter. 'You and I are real, Teddy, aren't we?'

The bear's eyes regarded the boy unflinchingly. 'You and I are real, David.' It specialised in comfort.

Monica walked slowly about the house. It was almost time for the afternoon post to come over the wire. She punched the O.L. number on the dial on her wrist but nothing came through. A few minutes more.

She could take up her painting. Or she could dial her friends. Or she could wait till Henry came home. Or she could go up and play with David . . .

She walked out into the hall and to the bottom of the stairs.

'David!'

No answer. She called again and a third time.

'Teddy!' she called, in sharper tones.

'Yes, Mummy!' After a moment's pause, Teddy's head of golden fur appeared at the top of the stairs.

'Is David in his room, Teddy?'

'David went into the garden, Mummy.'

'Come down here, Teddy!'

She stood impassively, watching the little furry figure as it climbed down from step to step on its stubby limbs. When it reached the bottom, she picked it up and carried it into the living-room. It lay unmoving in her arms, staring up at her. She could feel just the slightest vibration from its motor.

'Stand there, Teddy. I want to talk to you.' She set him down on a tabletop, and he stood as she requested, arms set forward and open in the eternal gesture of embrace.

'Teddy, did David tell you to tell me he had gone into the garden?'

The circuits of the bear's brain were too simple for artifice.

'Yes, Mummy.'

'So you lied to me.'

'Yes, Mummy.'

'Stop calling me Mummy! Why is David avoiding me? He's not afraid of me, is he?'

'No. He loves you.'

'Why can't we communicate?'

'Because David's upstairs.'

The answer stopped her dead. Why waste time talking to this machine? Why not simply go upstairs and scoop David into her arms and talk to him, as a loving mother should to a loving son? She heard the sheer weight of silence in the house, with a different quality of silence issuing from every room. On the upper landing, something was moving very silently – David, trying to hide away from her . . .

He was nearing the end of his speech now. The guests were attentive; so was the Press, lining two walls of the banqueting chamber, recording Henry's words and occasionally photographing him.

'Our serving-man will be, in many senses, a product of the computer. Without knowledge of the genome, we could never have worked through the sophisticated biochemics that go into synthetic flesh. The serving-man will also be an extension of the computer – for he will contain a computer in his own head, a microminiaturised computer capable of dealing with almost any situation he may encounter in the home. With reservations, of course.'

Laughter at this; many of those present knew the heated debate that had engulfed the Synthank boardroom before the decision had finally been taken to leave the serving-man neuter under his flawless uniform.

'Amid all the triumphs of our civilisation – yes, and amid the crushing problems of overpopulation too – it is sad to reflect how many millions of people suffer from increasing loneliness and isolation. Our serving-man will be a boon to them; he will always answer, and the most vapid conversation cannot bore him.

'For the future, we plan more models, male and female – some of them without the limitations of this first one, I promise you! – of more advanced design, true bio-electronic beings.

'Not only will they possess their own computers, capable of individual programming: they will be linked to the Ambient, the World Data Network. Thus everyone will be able to enjoy the equivalent of an Einstein in their own homes. Personal isolation will then be banished for ever!'

He sat down to enthusiastic applause. Even the synthetic serving-man, sitting at the table dressed in an unostentatious suit, applauded with gusto.

Dragging his satchel, David crept round the side of the house. He climbed on to the ornamental seat under the living-room window and peeped cautiously in.

His mother stood in the middle of the room. Her face was blank; its lack of expression scared him. He watched fascinated. He did not move; she did not move. Time might have stopped, as it had stopped in the garden. Teddy looked round, saw him, tumbled off the table, and came over to the window. Fumbling with his paws, he eventually got it open.

They looked at each other.

'I'm no good, Teddy. Let's run away!'

'You're a very good boy. Your mummy loves you.'

Slowly, he shook his head. 'If she loves me, then why can't I talk to her?'

'You're being silly, David. Mummy's lonely. That's why she has you.'

'She's got Daddy. I've got nobody 'cept you, and I'm lonely.'

Teddy gave him a friendly cuff over the head. 'If you feel so bad, you'd better go to the psychiatrist again.'

'I hate that old psychiatrist – he makes me feel I'm not real.' He started to run across the lawn. The bear toppled out of the window and followed as fast as its stubby legs would allow.

Monica Swinton was up in the nursery. She called to her son once and then stood there, undecided. All was silent.

Crayons lay on his desk. Obeying a sudden impulse, she went over to the desk and opened it. Dozens of pieces of paper lay inside. Many of them were written in crayon in David's clumsy writing, with each letter picked out in a colour different from the letter preceding it. None of the messages was finished.

MY DEAR MUMMY, HOW ARE YOU REALLY, DO YOU LOVE ME AS MUCH

DEAR MUMMY, I LOVE YOU AND DADDY AND THE SUN IS SHINING

DEAR DEAR MUMMY, TEDDY'S HELPING ME TO WRITE TO YOU. I LOVE YOU AND TEDDY

DARLING MUMMY, I'M YOUR ONE AND ONLY SON AND I LOVE YOU SO MUCH THAT SOME TIMES

DEAR MUMMY, YOUR REALLY MY MUMMY AND I HATE TEDDY

DARLING MUMMY, GUESS HOW MUCH I LOVE
DEAR MUMMY, I'M YOUR LITTLE BOY NOT TEDDY
AND I LOVE YOU BUT TEDDY
DEAR MUMMY, THIS IS A LETER TO YOU JUST TO
SAY HOW MUCH HOW EVER SO MUCH

Monica dropped the pieces of paper and burst out crying. In their gay inaccurate colours the letters fanned out and settled on the floor.

Henry Swinton caught the express in high spirits, and occasionally said a word to the synthetic serving-man he was taking home with him. The serving-man answered politely and punctually, although his answers were not always entirely relevant by human standards.

The Swintons lived in one of the ritziest city-blocks. Embedded in other apartments, their apartment had no windows on to the outside; nobody wanted to see the overcrowded external world. Henry unlocked the door with his retina-pattern-scanner and walked in, followed by the serving-man.

At once, Henry was surrounded by the friendly illusion of gardens set in eternal summer. It was amazing what Whologram could do to create huge mirages in small spaces. Behind its roses and wisteria stood their house: the deception was complete: a Georgian mansion appeared to welcome him.

'How do you like it?' he asked the serving-man.

'Roses occasionally suffer from black spot.'

'These roses are guaranteed free from any imperfections.'

'It is always advisable to purchase goods with guarantees, even if they cost slightly more.'

'Thanks for the information,' Henry said dryly. Synthetic life-forms were less than ten years old, the old android mechanicals less than sixteen; the faults of their systems were still being ironed out, year by year.

He opened the door and called to Monica.

She came out of the sitting-room immediately and flung her arms round him, kissing him ardently on cheek and lips. Henry was amazed.

Pulling back to look at her face, he saw how she seemed to generate light and beauty. It was months since he had seen her so excited. Instinctively, he clasped her tighter.

'Darling what's happened?'

'Henry, Henry – oh, my darling, I was in despair . . . But I've dialled the afternoon post and – you'll never believe it! Oh, it's wonderful!'

'For heaven's sake, woman, what's wonderful?'

He caught a glimpse of the heading on the stat in her hand, still warm from the wall-receiver: Ministry of Population. He felt the colour drain from his face in sudden shock and hope.

'Monica . . . oh . . . Don't tell me our number's come up!'

'Yes, my darling, yes, we've won this week's parenthood lottery! We can go ahead and conceive a child at once!'

He let out a yell of joy. They danced round the room. Pressure of population was such that reproduction had to be strictly controlled. Childbirth required government permission. For this moment they had waited four years. Incoherently they cried their delight.

They paused at last, gasping, and stood in the middle of the room to laugh at each other's happiness. When she had come down from the nursery, Monica had de-opaqued the windows, so that they now revealed the vista of garden beyond. Artificial sunlight was growing long and golden across the lawn – and David and Teddy were staring through the window at them.

Seeing their faces Henry and his wife grew serious.

'What do we do about *them*?' Henry asked.

'Teddy's no trouble. He works well enough.'

'Is David malfunctioning?'

'His verbal communication centre is still giving him trouble. I think he'll have to go back to the factory again.'

'Okay. We'll see how he does before the baby's born. Which reminds me – I have a surprise for you: help just when help is needed! Come into the hall and see what I've got.'

As the two adults disappeared from the room, boy and bear sat down beneath the standard roses.

'Teddy – I suppose Mummy and Daddy are real, aren't they?'

Teddy said, 'You ask such silly questions, David. Nobody knows what "real" really means. Let's go indoors.'

'First I'm going to have another rose!' Plucking a bright pink flower, he carried it with him into the house. It could lie on the pillow as he went to sleep. Its beauty and softness reminded him of Mummy.

Supertoys When
Winter Comes

In Mrs Henry Swinton's garden it was not always
summer. Monica had ventured out into the crowded
city with David and Teddy and bought a VRD for
'Eurowinter'. Now the almond trees were barren of leaves.
Their branches were loaded with snow. The snow would
never melt as long as the disk kept playing.

So on the fake walls and windows of the Swinton simulation house the snow would remain lodged for ever on
the windowsills. The icicles hanging from the gutters
would never melt as long as the disk kept playing.

The frosty blue winter sky would remain for ever the
same, as long as the disk kept playing.

David and Teddy were playing by the frozen ornamental
pond. Their game was simple. They slid from opposite
sides of the pond and narrowly missed each other as they
passed. This always caused them to laugh.

'I nearly hit you that time, Teddy!' David cried.

Monica watched from the window of her living room.
Bored by their repetitive actions, she switched the

window off and turned away. The synthetic serving-man hobbled forward from his alcove and enquired gravely if there was anything he could get her.

'No thank you, Jules.'

'I'm sorry to see you appear to be still grieving, ma'am.'

'It's quite all right, Jules. I shall get over it.'

'Perhaps you would like me to ask your friend Dora-Belle over?'

'That is not necessary.'

Henry Swinton had recently equipped the serving-man with an update. It had affected his walking skills, which were now less certain. It made him appear quite realistically as an older man, and so had not been corrected. He now spoke in a more human way, and Monica liked him better.

She called Henry on the Ambient. His face came up smiling in the globe.

'Monica, hi! How's tricks? It looks as if the take-over is going to happen. I'm due to talk to Havergail Bronzwick in nine minutes, EST. If we can clinch it, the deal will make Synthmania the biggest synthetics company on the planet, bigger than anything in Japan or the States.'

Monica listened alertly, although she realised her husband was mouthing a rehearsed speech he was about to deliver to Bronzwick.

'When I think where we've come from, Monica . . . If this deal goes through, I'll – we'll – immediately be three million mondos richer. I already have great plans for us. We'll move to a better place, sell off David and Teddy, get some of the new batch of synths, buy an island . . .'

'Will you be home soon?'

The question brought Henry's excited talk to a halt. He said cautiously, 'You know I have to be away this week. I hope to get back Monday . . .'

She switched off.

Sitting in her swivel chair, hands clasped, she caught a movement from the corner of her eye. David and Teddy were still sliding on the pool, giving their small cries of merriment. Perhaps they would continue for ever. She rose, pressing open the window, and called to them.

'Come in now, children. Go upstairs and play.'

'All right, Mummy!' David called. He climbed from the frozen pool, turning to help his clumsy friend over the plastoid lip.

'I'm getting so fat, David,' said Teddy. He laughed.

'You were always quite fat, Teddy. That's what I like about you,' said David. 'It makes you cuddly.'

They scampered through the front door, which squelched shut behind them. Upstairs they went, simulating jollity between them. 'I will race you!' David called to Teddy. It was so childlike. Monica saw with a certain melancholy their heels disappear between the bannisters.

The clock of her Ambient chimed five and switched on. She turned to the machine and was soon networking. All round the planet, other people, mainly women, began to discuss religious issues. Some despatched their electronic thoughts to arrive on paper. Others showed photomontages they had made.

'I need God because I am alone so frequently,' said Monica to the multitude. 'My baby died. But I don't know where God is. Maybe he doesn't visit cities.'

Answers poured in.

'Are you mad enough to think God lives a country existence? If so, forget it. God's everywhere.'

'God is only a prayer away, wherever you live. I will pray for you.'

'Of course you are alone. God is just a concept, invented

by an unhappy man. Get a life, darling. Check up on the neurosciences.'

'It's because you think you are alone that God cannot get to you!'

She worked through the answers, recording them, for two hours. Then she switched off the Ambient and sat in silence. Silence prevailed upstairs also.

One day, she was determined, she would make an analysis of all the messages she received. A synthesis would be valuable. She would compose an Amb-production of the results. Her name would become known. She would dare to walk – with a guard – in the city streets. People would say, 'Why, that's Monica Swinton!'

She shook herself from her daydream. Why was David so quiet?

David and Teddy were sprawling on the floor of their room together, looking at a vidbook. They giggled at the antics of the performing animals. A chubby little elephant in tartan trousers kept falling over a drum which rolled down a street towards a river.

'He is going to go in that river, sooner or later!' said Teddy, between chortles.

The pair of them looked up when Monica appeared. She stooped, picked up the book and snapped it shut.

'Haven't you tired of this toy yet?' she asked. 'You have had it for three years. You must know exactly what's going to happen to that silly little elephant.'

David hung his head, although he was used to his mother's disapproval.

'We just like what's going to happen, Mummy. I bet if we watch it again Elly will roll right into the river. It's so funny.'

'But we won't watch it if you don't want us to,' Teddy added.

She repented her outburst; after all, she knew their limitations. Setting the vidbook down on the carpet, she said with a sigh, 'You'll never grow up.'

'I am trying to grow up, Mummy. This morning, I watched a natural history science program on DTV.'

Monica said that that was good. She asked what David had learnt. He told her he had learnt about dolphins. 'We are part of the natural world, aren't we, Mummy?'

When he lifted up his arms to her for a cuddle, she backed away, her mind choked with the thought of being imprisoned for ever in an eternal childhood, never developing, never escaping . . .

'I expect Mummy's ever so busy,' said David to Teddy, when Monica had left.

They sat there, the two of them, looking at each other. Smiling.

Henry Swinton was dining with Petrushka Bronzwick. A couple of decorative blondes were accompanying them at the table. They were in a restaurant with an anachronistic live quartet playing nearby. Synthmania's friendly takeover of Havergail Bronzwick PLC was proceeding satisfactorily; lawyers were due to complete all documents by the day after the morrow.

Scene: a restaurant only for the wealthy. Boast: a real window in the ceiling, letting in summer light sullied only slightly by pollution.

Petrushka and Henry, with their ladies, were tucking in to two small sucking pigs, turning on spits beside their table. The pigs sizzled and dripped goodness. The diners washed everything down with vintage champagne.

'Oh, this is so good!' exclaimed the blonde who called herself Bubbles. She belonged to Petrushka Bronzwick. She mopped her chin with a lawn napkin. 'I could go on eating for ever, couldn't you?'

Leaning forward with knife and fork poised, Henry said, 'We have to keep ahead of the competition, Pet. Every cubic centimetre of the cerebral cortex in the human brain contains fifty million nerve cells. That's what we're up against, you realise. The day of synthetic brains is over and done. Forget it. We're manufacturing real brains from yesterday on.'

'Sure,' agreed Petrushka. She leaned forward to cut herself another slice of belly, waving away the waiter who came forward. 'Waiters are always so stingy in serving.' Her silvery laugh was famous, and dreaded in' some quarters. She was just into her twenties, already on Preservanex, spectrally thin, with short multi-coloured hair, blue eyes and a slight twitch in her left multi-coloured cheek. 'And we're talking one hundred million nerve cells. But since we junked silicon we're on our way to win out. The question, Henry, remains one of funding.'

Pushing a succulent mouthful into his face before replying, Henry said, 'Synthmania's Crosswell tape will take care of that little item. You've seen the figures. The GNP of Kurdistan is peanuts in comparison. Production is up again this year, fourteen per cent. Crosswell was our first big-selling line, back when we were Synthank. It's conquered the Western world. The Pill has nothing on the Crosswell.'

'Sure, I've got a Crosswell in me,' said Angel Pink. She pointed downwards to her lap with a dainty finger. She was the one Henry fancied. For emphasis, she added – sideways glance at Henry – 'it's in me all the time.'

Leaning towards her, Henry granted her a twinkle and one of his favourite spiels. 'Three-quarters of this over-populated world of ours are starving. We are lucky to have more than enough of everything, thanks to the capping of population-production. Obesity is our main problem, not malnutrition.'

'So so true!' sighed Bubbles. Red lips, white teeth, she champed on a golden strand of crackling.

'Is there anyone who doesn't have a Crosswell working for them in their small intestine?' Henry asked, shaking his head by way of answer to his own question. 'Jim Crosswell was a nanobiologist of genius. I was the one who found him, gave him a job. This safe parasitic worm enables anyone to eat up to one hundred per cent more food and still keep his or her figure, right?'

'Sure, one of yesterday's great inventions,' said Petrushka, looking spiteful. 'Our Senoram is just about as profitable.'

'Costs more for one thing,' said Bubbles, but her remark was drowned out by Angel Pink clapping her pretty little hands. 'We're going to make a killing!' She raised her glass. 'Here's to you two clever people!'

In responding to the toast, Henry wondered where she got the 'we' from. She would pay for that error. He would see to it.

Monica was about to go skiing. The synthetic serving-man accompanied her to the cabin installed in the callerium. He proffered his arm in a courteous manner. She accepted it. She loved that touch of grace. It evoked for her a distant half-forgotten childhood where there had been . . . She had forgotten what there had been. Perhaps a loving father?

Once in the cabin, she hooked up and dialled the 'Mountain Snow' picture. Immediately, down came the snow, blizzard force. Visibility was bad. She laboured uphill. It was scary. She was utterly alone. A rare tree was shrouded in white.

Once she gained the shelter, she went in and rested, panting, before strapping on her skis. The challenge was the cold, the remorseless elements. She had met it, beaten it. The snow storm was tapering off. Before plunging downhill, she set the mask on her face. In that great exhilarating rush, her body braced itself against the mad, the roaring, the furious, the insupportable air. Behind the mask, her mouth opened in a shriek of purest joy. This was freedom – this embrace of gravity!

It was over. She stood alone, naked, in the enclosing cubicle.

When she was dressed, she emerged. Time perhaps for a sip of vodka. She preferred the United Dairies Vodka, which came with milk ready mixed.

David and Teddy were standing there uneasily. 'We were only playing, Mummy,' said David.

'We didn't make a noise,' said Teddy. 'It was Jules made a noise, falling over.'

Turning, Monica saw Jules lying on the floor. His left leg was slowly kicking. In his fall, he had reached for support and brought down Monica's reproduction Kussinski of which she was proud – of which she always spoke whenever her friend Dora-Belle called. It lay shattered beside the serving-man's cranium. The cranium had split open, revealing the auditory and speech matrix.

As Monica fell to her knees beside the body, David said, 'It doesn't matter, Mummy. We were only playing when he tripped. He's only an android.'

'Yes, he's just an android, Mummy,' said Teddy. 'You can soon buy another.'

'Oh God! It's Jules. Poor Jules! He was a friend to me.' She pressed her hand to her face. She shed no tear.

'You can soon buy us another, Mummy,' said David. He timidly touched her shoulder.

She turned on him. 'And what do you think you are? You're only a little android yourself!'

As soon as the words were out, she regretted them. But David was emitting a kind of scream, among which words were entangled. 'Not . . . not an android . . . I'm real . . . real like Teddy . . . like you, Mummy . . . only you don't love me . . . my program . . . never loved me . . .' He ran in small circles and, when the words had given out, ran for the stairs, still emitting his kind of scream.

Teddy followed him. They disappeared from sight. Monica rose to her feet and stood trembling over the body of the serving-man. She covered her eyes with her hands. Her despair was not so easily shut out.

A series of crashes came from the rooms above. Monica went warily to investigate.

Teddy lay sprawled flat on the carpet, arms outstretched. David knelt over him. He had opened Teddy's tummy, and was investigating the complex mechanisms of its interior.

Teddy saw Monica's look of horror. 'It's all right, Mummy. I let David do it. We're trying to find out if we're real or just – urrrp—'

David had removed a plug from high in the bear's chest, near the stabiliser, where the heart's left ventricle would have been in a human.

'Poor Teddy! He's dead! He really was a machine. So that means—'

As he spoke, he was waving his arms uncontrollably.

He fell back, striking his face. It cracked, revealing plastic working beneath.

'David! David! Don't grieve! We can repair—'

'Stop speak!' He shouted the words forcibly as, jumping up, he rushed past her, fled from the room and leaped down the stairs. She stood over the inert teddy bear, listening to David crashing about below. Of course, she thought, his eyes can no longer focus on the same object. His poor little face has come apart.

Fearful, she approached the stairs. She must call Henry for help. Henry must return home.

A brilliant crackling sounded. The intense splutter of freed electricity. Dazzling light. Darkness.

'David!' But she was falling.

David had struck the house's control centre, wrenching it from the wall in a fury of pain and despair. Everything stopped playing.

The house disappeared, and the garden with it. David stood in the midst of a skeletal structure of wired scaffolding, bedded here and there in breeze blocks. Rubble lay underfoot. Acrid smoke drifted at ground level.

After a long stretch of immobility, he made his way forward, treading where the house had been, treading where the snowy garden had been, where he had played so often with his friend Teddy.

He stood in an alleyway, in an unknown world. Old pavement was slimy underfoot. Weeds grew between slabs. The detritus of an earlier epoch lay before him. He kicked a crushed can labelled 'oka-col'.

A drowsy light prevailed over all; the summer's day was coming to a close. He could not see clearly but, with his right eye, caught sight of a sickly rose growing by a crumbling brick wall.

Crossing to the plant, he plucked a bud. Its beauty and softness reminded him once more of Mummy.

Over her body he said, 'I am human, Mummy. I love you and I feel sad just like real people, so I must be human . . . Mustn't I?'

Supertoys in Other Seasons

Throwaway Town sprawled near the heart of the city. David made his way there, led by a large Fixer-Mixer. The Fixer-Mixer had many hands and arms of various dimensions. He kept them snugged down on his rusty carapace. Walking on extensible spider legs, he towered above David.

As they went along, David asked, 'Why are you so big?'

'The world's big, David. So I am big.'

After a silence, the five-year-old said, 'The world has been big since my Mummy died.'

'Machines don't have mummies.'

'I wish you to know I am not a machine.'

Throwaway was entered down a steep slope, and partly hidden from the going human world by a high wall of breeze-blocks. The road into this junk town was wide and easy. Everything inside was irregular. Strange shapes were the order of the day. Many shapes moved, or could move, or might move. Their colours were many, some sporting huge letters or numerals. Rusty brown was a favourite. They specialised in scratches, huge dents, shattered glass, broken panels. They stood in puddles and leaked rust.

This was the land of the obsolete. To Throwaway came or were dumped all the old models of automatics, robots, androids and other machines that had ceased to be useful to busy mankind. Here was everything that had once worked in some way, from toasters and electric carving knives to derricks and computers that could count only up to infinity-minus-one. The poor Fixer-Mixer had lost one of its grabbers and would never again haul a tonne of cement.

It was a town of a kind. Every junked object helped every other junked object. Every old-model pocket calculator could calculate something useful, if it was only how wide a lane should be left between two blocks of scrapped auto-mobilities to allow passage for wheelies and motormowers.

A tired old supermarket servitor took David into his care. They shared the burnt-out shell of a refrigeration unit.

'You'll be okay with me till your transistors blow,' the servitor said.

'You're very kind. I just wish I had Teddy with me,' said David.

'What was so special about Teddy?'

'We used to play together, Teddy and I.'

'Was he human?'

'He was like me.'

'Just a machine, eh? Better forget him, then.'

David thought to himself, Forget Teddy? I really loved Teddy. But it was quite cosy in the refrigeration unit.

One day the servitor asked, 'Who kept you?'

'I had a daddy called Henry Swinton. But he was generally away on business.'

*

24

Henry Swinton was away on business Together with three associates, he was ensconced in a hotel on an island in the South Seas. The suite in which they were gathered looked out over golden sands to the ocean. Tamarisks grew below the window, their fronds waving slightly in a breeze that took the sting from the tropical heat.

The murmur of waves breaking on the beach did not penetrate the triple glazing.

Henry and his associates sat with bottles of mineral water and notefiles in front of them. Henry's back was to the pleasant view.

Henry had fought his way up to Chief Executive of Worldsynth-Claws. He outranked the others at the table. Of these others, one in particular, Asda Dolorosaria, had elected herself to speak for the opposition.

'You've seen the figures, Henry. Your proposed Mars investment will not pay off in a century. Please be reasonable. Forget the crazy notion.'

Henry said, 'Reason is one thing, flair another, Asda. You know the amount of business we do in Central Asia. It's the area of the planet most like Mars. We have communications sewn up. Not a single mech there that does not come from our factories. I bought into Central Asia when no one else would touch it. You have to trust me on Mars.'

'Samsavvy is against your argument,' said dry-voiced Mauree Shilverstein. Samsavvy was the Supersoftputer Mk.V which in effect ran Worldsynth-Claws. 'Sorry. You're brilliant, but you know what Samsavvy says.' She offered an imitation of a smile. 'He says forget it.'

Henry opened his hands and placed his fingers together so that they formed an arch of wisdom.

'Okay. But Samsavvy doesn't have my intuition. I intuit

that if we get our synthelp on Mars right now, they can run the atmosphere-maker. In no time – well, in half a century, let's say – Worldsynth will get to *own* the atmosphere. That's as good as owning Mars itself. All human activities are secondary to breathing, okay? Can't you people understand that?' He thumped the guaranteed real reconstituted wood table. 'You got to have flair. I built this whole enterprise on flair.'

Old Ainsworth Clawsinski had said nothing, contenting himself with an unwavering glare at Henry. He was the Claws of the company. The plug in his left ear indicated that he was in constant touch with Samsavvy. Now he spoke from his end of the table.

'Fuck your flair, Henry.'

His colleagues, encouraged, came in in chorus.

'Shareholders don't think in half-centuries, Henry,' said Mauree Shilverstein. She was the one who had initially inclined towards Henry's argument.

'Mars has no investment value. It's proved,' said Asda Dolorosaria. 'They've gotten in Tibetan labour. It's cheaper and it's expendable. Better forget about other planets, Henry, and concentrate that mind of yours on last year's two per cent profit dip on this planet.'

Henry went red.

'Forget the past. You're dragging your heels, all three of you! Mars is the future. Ainsworth, with all due respect, you're too damned old to even think about the future! We will adjourn and meet again at three thirty. Be warned – I know what I'm doing. I want Mars on a plate.'

Gathering up his pad, he marched out of the room.

David found that Throwaway had a We Mend You workshop. Through the maze of rusty alleyways he went, until he came to the workshop. It was situated in a static water-tank, turned upside down, with an entrance cut in its side by a welder. Inside this echoing shelter, industrious little machines worked and patched and sawed and rejoined. Still valid circuits were cannibalised, motors regenerated, the old made less old, the antiquated merely old.

And there David had his broken face repaired.

There too he met the Dancing Devlins. A socket in the male Devlin's leg had become displaced. Consumer society had scrapped him. Besides, he and his female machine, with their rapid dancing act, had become passé. They had been earning less money. They were junked.

The socket was replaced. Batteries were recharged.

Now Devlin (M) could dance again with Devlin (F). They took David with them to their tiny hovel. There they performed their lightning dance over and over. David watched and watched. He never tired of the routine.

'Aren't we wonderful, dear?' said Devlin (F).

'I would like it even more if only Teddy could watch with me.'

'It's the same dance, lad, whether Teddy is here or not.'

'But you don't understand . . .'

'I understand our dance is clever even if nobody is watching. Once hundreds of real people used to watch us dancing. But it was different then.'

'It's different now,' David said.

The sand was yielding underfoot. Henry Swinton kicked his trainers off and left them lying on the beach. He walked on the margins of the ocean. He was in a state of despair. He had fallen from a high cliff of success.

After the dismal outcome of the morning's meeting, he had gone to the residents' bar to enjoy a long slow vodkamilk, the Drink of the Year. 'Vodkakamilk – Smooth as Silk'. His associates had given him a wide berth. He had then taken an elevator up to his private penthouse on the top floor.

Peaches had gone. Her cases had gone.

Her fragrance lingered, not yet wiped out by the aircond.

On the mirror she had scrawled in lipstick READ YOUR AMBIENT!!! SORRY AND GOODBYE! P

'She's being funny,' thought Henry, aloud. He knew she was not. Peaches was never funny.

The Ambient was already tuned to the private Worldsynth channel. Henry crossed to the globe and turned it on.

SS MV.V. MESSAGE TO HENRY SWINTON. YOUR MARS GAMBLE NOT ACCEPTABLE TO SHAREHOLDERS. YOUR PROJECTS SURPLUS TO OUR FUTURE PLANS.

PLEASE ACCEPT THANKS AND INSTANT RETIREMENT HEREWITH. OPEN TO NEGOTIATION ON FINAL HANDSHAKE VALUE IF NO ARGUMENT FORTHCOMING. SEE EMPLOYMENT ACT 21066A CLAUSES 16–21. FAREWELL.

The ocean that had looked so bright and pure from the hotel was spewing up plastic bottles along the shoreline, together with dead fish. Henry finally flung himself down on the sand, exhausted. He had put on weight recently, despite his Crosswell tape, and was unaccustomed to walking.

No seagull had ever visited this island. Swallows abounded. The birds circled overhead, occasionally swooping on an insect in flight. Once an insect was caught, the bird returned with it to the eaves of the hotel to feed its young, screaming in their nest. Then it was back, fluttering above the decay where ocean met shore. There seemed to be no rest for the birds.

From Henry's low view, the hotel presented a rakish aspect. It had been built on sand. Slowly, one end was sinking down. It resembled a vast concrete ship in trouble in a sepia sea.

He endured a rage of hatred about everyone he knew, everyone who had crossed his path from the beginning. The low rumble of plastic bottle bumping against plastic bottle formed an accompaniment to his anger.

He contemplated killing Ainsworth Clawsinski, for some while his enemy on the board. Eventually the anger turned against himself.

'But what have I done? What have I been? What's been in my mind? A big success! Empty success . . . Yes, empty. I've just sold things. I'm a salesman, nothing more. Or I *was* a salesman. Buying and selling. My God, I wanted to buy *Mars*. A whole planet . . . I have been mad with greed. I am mad. I'm sick, mortally sick. What did I ever care about?

'I have never been creative. I imagined I was creative. I've never been a scientist. I'm just a smartass. What do I really understand about the mechs I sell . . . Oh God, what a failure I am, a desperate failure. Now I've gone too far. Why didn't I see? Why did I neglect Monica? Monica, my darling . . . Monica, I did love you. And I fobbed you off with a toy kid. Kids. David and Teddy.

'Huh. At least David loved you. David. Poor little toy David, your one consolation.

'My God, whatever happened to David? Maybe . . .'

The swallows screamed overhead.

*

A council truck came slowly down the wide road into Throwaway Town. Once inside the gates, it turned its massive nose left, entering what was known as Dump Place.

Automatics began slowly to tip the rear platform. A number of obsolete robots, which had long served the public working in the subway system, slid from the back of the truck. They crashed to the ground. The truck scraped the last robot, clinging to the rear board, off on to the dump.

One or two of the robots were broken in the fall. One lay on its face, helplessly waving an arm until another mech helped it up. Together they made off into the depths of the rusty aisles.

David ran up to see the excitement. The Dancing Devlins ceased their dance to follow him.

When the other newly arrived robots had gone, one still remained. It sat in the dirt shooting its arms back and forth in a prescribed pattern.

Going as close as he dared, David asked the mech why he did that.

'I still work, don't I? Don't I still work? I can work in the dark but my lamp is broken. My lamp will not work. I hit my lamp on a girder overhead. There was a girder overhead. I hit my lamp on it. The chief computer sent me here. I still work.'

'What did you do? Were you on the subway?'

'I worked. I worked well since I was built. I still work.'

'I never did any work. I played with Teddy. Teddy was my friend.'

'Have you any instructions? I work still, don't I?'

While this conversation was in progress, a sleek black limo entered Throwaway. A man was sitting in the front seat. Spinning the window down, he stuck his head out and asked something.

What he said was, 'David? Are you David Swinton?'

David went over to the auto. 'Daddy? Oh, Daddy, have you really come for me? I don't really belong here in Throwaway.'

'Climb in, David. We'll get you all cleaned up for Monica's sake.'

David looked round. The Dancing Devlins stood nearby. They were not dancing. David called out a goodbye to them. The Dancing Devlins simply stood where they were. They had never been programmed to say goodbye. It was not quite the same as taking a bow.

As David climbed into his father's car, they began to perform their dance. It was their favourite dance. It was the dance they had performed a hundred thousand times before.

Henry Swinton was no longer rich. He no longer had a career. He no longer had women around. He no longer had ambition.

But he had time.

He sat in a cheap apartment on Riverside, talking to David. The apartment was old and worn. One of the walls had developed a stammer. Sometimes it showed a false view of the river, where the water was blue and old-fashioned paddle-steamers bedecked with flags plied up and down. Sometimes it showed a commercial for Preservanex, where a couple in their early hundreds went through rickety copulation movements.

'How can I not be human, Daddy? I'm not like the Dancing Devlins or the other people I met in Throwaway. I feel happy or sad. I love people. Therefore I am human. Isn't that so?'

'You won't understand this, David, but I'm a broken man. I've fouled up my whole life. The way people do.'

'My life was nice when we lived in that house with Mummy.'

'I said you wouldn't understand.'

'I do understand, Daddy. Can we go back there?'

Henry gazed mournfully at the five-year-old standing before him, a half-smile on his scarred face. 'There's never any going back.'

'We could go back in the limo.'

Henry seized the boy and held him tightly, arms wrapped around him. 'David, you were an early product of my first mech company, Synthank. You have since been superseded. You only think you are happy or sad. You only think you loved Teddy or Monica.'

'Did you love Monica, Daddy?'

He sighed heavily. 'I thought I did.'

Henry put David in the auto, telling him that his obsession with being human would count as a neurosis if he were human. There were humans who had illnesses where they imagined they were machines.

'I'll show you.'

From the ruins of Henry Swinton's career, little remained. One thing, however, did remain. There still survived, out in a rundown suburb between city and boonies, the production unit of Synthank, Henry's first enterprise, which had not been swallowed up in his increasingly megalomaniac dreams.

He had retained financial control of Synthank. And its products had not been destroyed. They survived on a low level of production, supervised by Henry's old human friend, Ivan Shiggle. Shiggle exported Synthank's products to undeveloped countries overseas where, in their simplicity, they were welcomed as additional labour.

'We could insert better brains in them. Then they would be more up-to-date. But why go to the expense?' said Henry, as he and the boy turned into the unit's yard.

'They might like to have better brains,' David suggested. Henry merely laughed.

Shiggle came out to meet them. Shaking hands with Henry, he looked down on David. 'An early model,' he remarked. 'What did Monica think of it?'

Henry took his time in responding. As they entered the building, he said, 'You know, Monica was rather a cold woman.'

Shooting him a sympathetic glance, Shiggle said, 'But you married her? You loved her?' Lights came on as they walked along a corridor and through a swing glass door. David followed meekly.

'Oh yes, I loved Monica. Not well enough. Perhaps she didn't love me well enough. I don't know. My ambition got the better of me – she must have found me hard to live with. Now she's dead – through my neglect. My life is a complete cock-up, Ivan.'

'You're not the only one. What have I done with my life? I often ask myself that.'

Henry clapped his friend on his shoulder. 'You've been a good friend of mine. You have never cheated me or turned against me.'

'There's time yet,' said Shiggle, and both men laughed.

They had gained the production floor, where the product stood ready for packaging and exporting. David came forward, staring, his eyes wide.

He confronted a thousand Davids. All looking alike. All

dressed alike. All standing alert and alike. All silent, staring ahead. A thousand replicas of himself. Unliving.

For the first time David really understood.

This was what he was. A product. Only a product. His mouth fell open. He froze. He could not move. The gyroscope ceased within him. He fell backwards to the floor.

On the afternoon of the following day, Shiggle and Henry stood in their shirtsleeves. They grinned at each other and shook hands.

'I still know how to work, Ivan! Amazing! Maybe there's hope for me yet.'

'You can have a job here. We'd get on okay together. Provided the neural brain works in this son of yours.'

David lay on the bench between them still connected by a cable, awaiting rebirth. His clothes had been renewed from stock, his face had been properly remoulded. And the later type of brain had been inserted, infused with his earlier memories.

He had been dead. Now was the time to see if he would live again, and would enjoy a brain many times more diverse in its powers than his old one.

The two men ceased their casual conversation. They paused over the prostrate body.

Henry turned to the figure standing by their side, its arms wide in the eternal gesture of love and welcome.

'Are you ready for this, Teddy?'

'Yes, I am very excited to play with David again,' said the bear. He was one of a stock of bears held in the production unit, primed with memory-rerun. 'I missed him very much. David and I used to have such fun together, once.'

'That's good. Well, then, let's bring David back to life, shall we?'

Yet still the men hesitated. They had done manually what was generally performed automatically.

Teddy beamed. 'Hooray! Where we lived before it was always summer. Until the end. Then it was winter.'

'Well, it's spring now,' said Shiggle. Henry hit the charge button. The figure of David jerked. His right hand automatically pulled away the connecting cable. He opened his eyes.

He sat up. His hands went up to his head. His expression was one of amazement. 'Daddy! What a strange dream I had. I never had a dream before . . .'

'Welcome back, David, my boy,' said Henry.

Embracing the child, he lifted David off the bench. David and Teddy stared at each other in wonder. Then they fell into each other's arms.

It was almost human.

Apogee Again

I don't know if you'll believe this but there was a time when I lived in a different world. Much like ours but just a little different.

One different thing was the way the female sex behaved. But then, as we always expected, the women had wings and could fly. The wings were not like angels' wings: more like a peacock's tail, fragile-seeming, many-coloured, in hues which caught and reflected the sunlight. And were enormous: the length of a bruiseball patch. Oh, the women looked so lovely as they flew naked overhead. Young men had been known to die from the shock of the beauty of it.

Because of the nature of their diet, their droppings were light and floated gently to the ground, almost defying gravity.

The women lived at the top of great hollow columns, I should mention. No one knew how ancient were the columns; nor would anyone knowing have been believed. These were the columns supporting the high platforms. Females young and old flew from one huge aerial platform to another – to those huge platforms where no men were allowed to set foot. Of course, as I shall relate, the flying women would come down to ground level on occasions. Some of them got married to men. On their wedding day, or when they lost their virginity, whichever came sooner, the feathers fell from their wings. The wing structures withered and died. And from that day forth, the married woman had to walk everywhere. And behave like an ordinary person, who cannot possibly imagine taking flight. There was, at the time of which I am speaking, when the world was growing darker, and the sun shrinking, a saying among men: 'If the Hallon had meant us to fly, she would not have given us testicles'.

The men who lived on the ground had no beliefs. Even the idea of there being a Hallon had come from the women. They lived by the day, which meant they found it hard to imagine anything that was not in front of their eyes. But the women had a faith, and a rather ridiculous one, full of bizarre imaginings.

The women clutched their genitals as they recited: 'I believe that our brief life is not all. I believe that after our lives are over, the darkness will live. I believe that dragons will fly and will eat us all, every bit of us, including those useful parts of which we have hold.'

Delicious shivers overcame them as they recited this mantra each day at evenfall. For they both believed and did not believe. The idea of flying dragons sounded so – well, dear, preposterous, really.

Of course the women had many other things to preoccupy them. Singing was practically a martial art. Wing-preening took up much time. Flap-motion was a daily exercise. It was said that by night two women, working together, would swoop down on an unsuspecting man and fly with him back to their platform, where they shared him. On such occasions, their wings did not perish.

Women sang their happiness above the ground. Men could catch the faint strains. Some men had died from love of the music. Large amplifiers of beaten tin had been invented, so that the music could be heard more clearly. The amplifiers were the trade of the Amplificers.

Heatmaker was a poor occupation. No one could invent fire, since flames could not tolerate our complex atmosphere.

The favoured trade at ground level on our planet was that of Upwardsman. The Upwardsmen were perpetually creating false wings, which the purchaser could attach to himself and attempt to fly up to the platforms. Anything to capture one of those winged beauties! So far, only young Dedlukki had succeeded. Others had managed to hover on a level with the platforms, only to have the women repel them with poles until, worn out from flapping their arms, they plunged to their deaths on the ground far below.

So the women flew free, enjoying the breezes, and the men laboured, or tended their herds. The women flew free, against a turquoise sky that was slowly changing colour, month by month, into a more ominous grey, and the grey into a dull red. The women flew free while warmth was gradually giving way to cold.

Upwardsman Wissler was a man who knew a little about such things. Wissler it was who called a council and first declared that what he called Glowbal Kooling was taking place, and that the time would come when the atmosphere would freeze unless – ah, but unless *what*? The matter was much debated.

Finally, it was decided that the women should be consulted on the matter. The great tin amplifiers were turned about. The women were addressed from below to on high.

'Beautiful ladies, we are subject to terrible changes in our world. The Glowbal sun goes ever further away. Before it reaches maximum distance, most of our air will become as ocean. So the wise men say.

'And the wise men talk of dragons devouring the world.

'How may we restore heat to our lands? Only by the heat of our bodies. We therefore humbly petition you that you permit a number of our young and handsome men to climb up the two thousand steps concealed within your columns and enter your platforms. There they will cohabit with you and, by pressing their pegos into your gorgeous lars, enter into fornication with you. The friction from which will return heat to our suffering world. Tell us, pray, that you accept this offer.'

Silvery laughter came back from the upper world. Derisive voices called out in mockery. Some said, 'Good try, you fool men! You don't fool us!' Others called, 'We are not having you lot up here! No way!'

So the men returned to minding their sheapp and cahows.

The weather grew colder. Our atmosphere was composed of four main gases. The gas we called aspargo became agitated. Strange storms arose. Although aspargo is not breathable on its own, it seemed to ease our breathing. Now it was rising, so that ground level breathing became disorderly. The colder it grew, the higher the aspargo rose.

As for the women in the upper world, being naked they suffered greatly. Their beautiful wings lost lustre. Feathers were shed until most of them were unable to fly. Finally, when the sky seemed to have turned red for ever, and a strange mist prevailed, an older woman who still retained her wings flew down to the ground and called forth Upwardsman Wissler and others.

When she addressed the assembled crowd, she said, 'I speak for the majority of our women. We have observed that the air grows colder and harder to breathe. We therefore propose that we come down to your level to present our lars to your pegos, that mass intercourse may take place, so that the heat generated will return our planet to the happy state in which it previously was.

'We are aware that this action may seem unpleasant, but can see no other course to take. Your young men must do their duty for the good of the race.'

She showed no surprise when the youths agreed readily to this proposal. Many strode forward to volunteer. They confessed that their pegos were already on the alert to do their duty in entering various lars.

A day was arranged, and that rather hurriedly, since the increased cold threatened to produce a terrible lethargy. The sun was now little more than a frozen eyeball, diminished under its eyelid of eclipsing cloud. The men were in dismay, for already some of the animals on which their livelihood depended had gone into a strange catalepsy from which it proved impossible to awaken them.

The women, on the agreed day, climbed down the two thousand steps inside their great columns. None was able to fly. Their useless wings scraped against the interior walls as they descended. Hanging overhead, on the undersides of the great steps, were large snail-like objects. These stirred as the women were passing. One or two even put out crisp prawn antennae which waved about, as if keeping the downward procession under scrutiny.

To the women, the ground seemed very dark. Some were afraid. The men greeted them with torches filled with firebirds, although it was noted that no longer did the torches gleam brightly as once they had done. The dull things, however, sufficed for the men to lead the women into their Grand Hall, where forty rough beds had been laid out, spread with gaudy rugs, twenty to each side of the hall, with a narrow space in the middle down which everyone could walk to take up their positions.

Most of the women had lengths of cloth wrapped about their bodies for warmth. While they divested themselves of these cloths, the men were hurriedly removing their own crude garb. They presented themselves to their partners. Some of the pegos were already alert. Others needed a little coaxing. A gong was struck – its note slightly flat. The eighty partners got down on the beds and lay beside each other. They kissed and felt each other's principle parts, such as pegos, lars and tutties.

At another stroke of the gong, mass fornication commenced.

Eighty bottoms moved as one. A slurping sound filled the chamber. Much excitement and warmth was generated. Indeed, as the awestruck superintendent remarked afterwards, 'Enough semen was generated to fill enough mijlk-bottles to feed all the cahows on the planet.' The logic of the remark hardly stands up under examination, unlike the pegos involved.

Towards the end of this day-long event, the men found that they were preferring immobility. A neuroleptic effect was taking place. Buttock after buttock ceased to move, became as unmoving as a carving. The women disengaged themselves and stood up with difficulty, for they too found themselves verging on the side of immobility. They

climbed over the inert bodies of the men and left the great
Hall of Recreation and Copulation. There a strange
prospect met their half-closed eyes.

A deep blue haze, nearly as thick as treacle, covered the
ground, almost up to knee-high, and rising. The air was a
blur of snowflakes, and full of strange noises, some rude,
some musical. The atmosphere was precipitating out.
Clutching each other for support, in many cases with their
body-wrapping flapping in the wind far behind them, the
women made their way back to their pillars.

They struggled to enter, struggled to mount a few steps,
before a strange catalepsy seized them. The last woman to
enter, glancing upwards, saw through a gap in the cloud
that their once friendly sun was now but a distant spark.

'We got it wrong,' she gasped. 'Thank Hallon!'

Now the phenomena of apogee increased, speeded up,
as if the next perihelion were not several thousand years
away in the future.

Like a lamp in the tormented sky, the moon went out. It
failed to illumine. It rolled dead in its orbit. And the snow
that fell came down in long twirling rods instead of individual flakes. The deep blue haze became deeper, and
turned into fluid as it deepened. Within a few hours, even
the great Hall of Recreation and Copulation was inun-
dated. Only its roof showed above the flood. Then the roof
itself sank beneath sullen waves. No great cry emerged
from the throat of any man: all had become in love with
darkness and submergence and the voracious silences of
eternity. And still it rained. And the flood rose up the
sides of the columns.

And what of the women inside those columns?

The changeover in atmosphere reduced them to
catalepsy, there on the great steps. They curled together in

parodies of some ethnic disaster, became solid. Lungs ceased to move, hearts to beat, blood to travel. Their wombs, those receptacles of a far future, became porcelain. And what was contained within that porcelain chamber was a tiny patient thing, a mere multiplicity of cells, content to wait through centuries of chill and dark, until once more planet and primary sailed into centuries of contiguity.

Above these heaps of mummified motherhood, the shells hanging from the underside of steps showed movement. Things were stirring, awakening from a long phylogenic dream in which night was day and day night, and all dimensions were contained within a shrimp's scrotum.

Now the shrimps were roused, and carried, still half a-doze, upwards through the flooding cylinders – finally to burst in glory upon their fine revived environment, all glooming dark and refreshing espargo air. Espargo, with its low freeze-point, skittered on new winds above a great brimming sea, which occasionally splashed and broke on the platforms.

All below them was an ocean of old atmosphere. All above them was the magnificent cloak of stars, as if the galaxy were ablaze with newly kindled flame. There was fire indeed, turned to diamonds . . .

Their whiskers grew at the sight and smell of it. Their bodies stretched like elastic stockings. Their many legs took on height and muscle and activity. Colour rippled along their hollow bodies. They ran squealing in happiness, rejoicing in the privilege of being alive, conscious – *airborne*. As they ran, their wings blossomed out like giant flowers, spreading, beating, flapping kite-like, carrying their fragile bodies into the merry dark espargo.

When their bodies lifted, so did their spirits. The espargo was alight with hastening colour.

There they sailed, the negative race, free of information, free of knowledge, free of any wisdom but the wisdom of sailing on the winds above the ocean – that atmosphere which was to remain ocean for thousands of years – to scatter their seed in great scented streamers on the icy zephyrs, until the solar dawn broke, and once more returning sunlight performed its duties for the creatures that existed blindly below the atmospheric ocean.

Neither species knew the other. Each had its turn of happiness. To each, the other species was but a dream.

As I said, this world was much like ours, only a little different.

III

Good evening. I am speaking to you as the visual representative of the III, late San Mondesancto Liquefaction Company, the legal owners of the satellite Europa, the most valuable property in the Jupiter area of our solar system.

The illustrious history of our company goes back a long way. As you will know, San Mondesancto was founded on Earth in 1990. We have always been a company of high integrity, as well as believers in free trade. At the time of our founding, when we took over the Shanghai and Orient Banking Systems, an approaching crisis in the form of a global water shortage had scarcely 'hit the headlines', as we used to say. It was, of course, known to many government agencies in the developed nations of the world. We laid our plans accordingly.

During that early period, NASA made a remarkable discovery. NASA, I should remind you, stood for the National Aeronautics and Space Administration. It was the predecessor of the III, our International Interplanetary Industries. NASA's Lunar Prospector Mission detected millions of tonnes of ice at the lunar polar regions.

'Within the limited technologies of the time, there was no way that these ice fields could be exploited. This was where the genius of San Mondesancto entered. By judicious investment through various holding companies, we established a small fleet of remotely operated space-faring vehicles. Without human freight, the space-vehicles were comparatively cheap to run, and were soon installed above both lunar poles. Pumping stations went immediately into operation, drilling to depths of twenty-three metres.

The terrestrial shortage of fresh water was meanwhile taking hold. Many areas in previously fertile nations were reduced to drought or semi-drought conditions, while, more importantly, the industry of wealthy nations was impeded.

San Mondesancto offered to supply Earth's G7 nations with an initial two million tonnes of fresh fossil water per week, delivered in solid form, in exchange for pumping rights in desalination plants over the rest of the world. By a series of ambitious deals, the company gained control over Earth's primary water supplies. The operator here was our subsidiary, Tubulability plc.

Through another of our subsidiary companies, Aerial Irrigations Inc., a successful strategy of cloud-ionisation permitted us ninety-one per cent control of precipitation from the air. An early victory was the inhibition of annual monsoons, which could reduce the underlying countries to desert conditions, unless prosperous countries such as India paid a marginal fee of a few million rupees per year.

Operating unusual caution and exerting only democratic and capitalist principles, San Mondesancto had, by the middle of last century, virtually complete control over all terrestrial climates.

However, the company's plans were much more ambitious. We have always prided ourselves on our far-sightedness.

It was perceived from the very beginning of our operations on the Moon that the ice locked there offered immense benefits for the future conquest of the solar system. There, San Mondesancto has always been among the foremost developers, operating under the name International Interplanetary Industries. Many of the best young men and women and androids have been proud to join the San Mondesancto ranks.

Unusual living organisms, some multi-celled, had been discovered in the lunar icefields. These had been quietly exterminated, so that progress and development were not impeded. A few of our top company scientists, however, had observed that these tokens of alien life held the promise of other aliens existing on other astronomical bodies, which could be utilised as foodstuffs in future ventures.

From the lunar H_2O, a process of hydrolysis separated the oxygen and hydrogen. The hydrogen provided an essential for rocket fuel. The oxygen provided breathable atmosphere for vehicles with two-man crews. These vehicles, using the planet Mars as a slingshot operation, made the long haul away from Earth to Jupiter. It has always been a source of pride that San Mondesancto ships were the first to arrive on the satellite Europa. Our slogan, 'San Mondesancto Got There First', dates from that time. True, one crew was lost from the ice floes, but the other two crews survived to make good the claim.

Preliminary reconnaissance of this moon confirmed that beneath Europa's broken and icy surface lay a global ocean. Sonic measurements indicated that this ocean was fifteen to eighteen kilometres deep in places. Moreover,

the gravitational effect of the great striped gas planet looming in Europa's skies had caused the ocean to warm
considerably.

Cracks and chasms between the ice floes showed a
teeming life of krill-like creatures, barely two millimetres
long. When cooked and cautiously tasted, they proved
edible, if rather flavourless. During this food trial, a large
head burst through the ice. It was streamlined, its fur was
thick and white, with mobile pink nostrils. Its whiskers
were long. The general impression was of a dolphin
crossed with a kitten.

A report at the time – censored because it was uncon-
firmed and inconvenient – said that the creature tapped
on the ice as if signalling. It did not stay because to remain
in airless conditions would have proved lethal.

The San Mondesancto crew became alert. One man,
armed, was venturing out to inspect the beast closely, but
it disappeared with a swirl of water before he could capture it.

They called the brute a *splunger*, and the name has
stuck.

That incident marks the modest beginning of operations
for what has become our foremost company, Canquistador.
Within five years, it had become the biggest cannery company in the entire system, bar none.

We still speak of splungers, although they are now
extinct. Unfortunately, they were over-fished, along with
other denizens of the Europan deep. Nevertheless,
splungers and krill fed many brave explorers of the far
reaches of the solar system, as well as the factory slaves on
Mars.

During this period, San Mondesancto's name became
widely reviled among an ill-informed public. In order to

establish better relations, the name of our founding company was phased out. Henceforth, we have become better known as III, the International Interplanetary Industries.

Not until Triton, the moon of Neptune, was reached, was another source of food discovered. This again was an III discovery. The *flabbers* clearly had a language of sorts, with which they endeavoured to communicate, although their I.Q. was regarded as low. It was only later that their extraordinary city, known to men as Ultimate City, was found. Intelligent or not, the flabbers were certainly tasty, and greatly benefited mankind – thanks to III's mighty sub-division, Canquistador.

Now the first III starship, under the logo III, is being launched from the orbit of Pluto. It will carry mankind's civilisation into the galaxy – and the name and fame of III to the very stars themselves.

Thank you for listening, ladies and gentlemen.

THE OLD
MYTHOLOGY

The seepers weebed down on the tall sides of every urbhive. Hundreds, thousands, ceased their scootering to gaze upwards in delight, envy or catatonia at the radiant female face glowing on their windowfree walls. The entire urbstack was alight with the eyes, the pert nose, the pink gums and immaculate teeth of DoraDeen Englaston.

She spoke.

'Soon I will become Day – just plain Day! I am just so excited because of all this and this luck that has just happened to me. Here we are on the very first day of the wonderful twenty-second century and I have won – lucky me! – the just first prize in the competition.

'My prize is that I just get to be projected on the TDP, the fantabulous Temporal Displacement Projector – wow!'

Zoom zoom, went the mecheye until it was almost lost between those tender red lips, cosying up to the epic epiglottis.

'The TDP is just going to send me back to any place in time I choose, when I will wind up in the character of a chosen person of the chosen period. Isn't that just cute? The machine is switching on right now.'

DoraDeen had been an actor in a supersoap. There was hardly a sincere bone left in her body. That body now began to writhe as the TDP gained power.

'Golly gosh, it feels so strange. I'm definitely on my way now . . .' The event horizons of past time fluttered past her. 'Oh yes . . . Why, there just goes the British Empire. And . . . golly gosh, the Romans! Greece! Who are they? The Cythians? Never heard of Cythians . . .'

Her voice was fainter now, her image on the urbstack walls smaller.

'Oh, am I glad to escape the horrors of my own century – the commercialism, the shootings, the hair dyes, the drugs – and above all else, just the miseries of family life. Wow, that's why I'm going back to the Eolithic, when the world was new, before we weebed at all.

'I want to belong to an ordinary decent Stone-Age family, with a kind father and lots of affectionate siblings. There's a new just horizon ahead . . . bounding with love and simple old-fashioned family values . . .'

DoraDeen's voice faded. Below, scooting resumed.

All about stretched a great forest. No man could tell where lay its limits. The great trees ran until, rank on rank, they reached the oceans.

Here and there small communities had been established. In one community, pigs rooted and grunted, tied by their legs to stakes. Their lives were as frugal as those of their human captors. They chuntered their dislike of domesticity.

Where once this clearing stood is now a place of highways sweeping into the distance, filling stations and gigantic urbstacks. The butterflies have gone, together with the little blue-eyed flowers. Much has changed – but not the family life that DoraDeen craved.

Harmon preened himself in preparation for the feast. His sons had announced this feast to be a celebration of his power. He trimmed his whiskers with the edge of a shell. He anointed his shoulders with oil crushed from a rare herb. He secured a bright feather in his hair. He put on a new gown, tying it so that it covered his stomach and lower regions. He looked every inch a lord.

Then he set forth, walking stiffly.

Clouds loomed overhead. The day was as yet hardly spent. The Sun God had spread layers of mist to hang close to the ground. The mists curled away as Harmon progressed through them towards the meeting ground. Constant bird song was interrupted by a distant bugle note.

In the clearing, a wooden throne had been erected. Harmon's three daughters were taking up positions by the throne, decoratively on either side of it. The daughters were young and scantily clad. In the elaborately dressed hair of their heads they wore orange flowers, and in the hair upon their mounds of Venus, one wore small blue flowers and the second small red flowers. And the third, Day, wore a sprig of laurel in the vital places.

The dark daughter was by name Via, the fair one Roa. They beckoned to their father with formal waves of their hands. So did brunette Day, a little uncertainly, for she had once been DoraDeen, so long ago it seemed like a fairy tale.

Harmon paused. Scenting danger, he gripped more firmly the staff he carried. He looked about him, moving his old shaggy head from side to side. There seemed no reason for alarm.

Slowly, he approached the throne. His kissed first Roa, then Via, then Day, on their cheeks. The girls expressed no emotion; only Day thought to herself, 'This is just fun! Wow, back in the Stone Age with my new sisters! I'm already getting into character.' They inclined their faces to receive his prickly old kisses. Harmon gathered the folds of his robe about him, and seated himself on the throne — which until recently had been a log.

The bugle note sounded again.

He spoke with a hint of impatience to his daughters. 'Where is the feast to which my sons invited me?'

'Wait a little, Father,' said Roa. 'Try to be patient.'

'You will soon get all you deserve, Father,' said Via.

'Just something's bound to happen,' thought Day. She gave a little wriggle.

From different parts of the great forest, three youths emerged. They carried in outstretched arms before them, in the gesture of those bearing gifts, a sword, a dagger and an axe.

He who carried the sword was by name Woundrel.

He who carried the dagger was by name Cedred.

He who carried the axe was by name Aledref.

Aledref, Cedred and Woundrel came dressed only in loin-skirts, with horned black leather caps on their heads. Aledref carried a bugle slung over one shoulder. These were the sons of Harmon, young, ferocious, alert.

They approached their father. Their weapons they laid by their own feet. They bowed to Harmon, who received them with courtesy.

'So, my sons, I greet you warmly,' growled Harmon, looking more displeased than his words might suggest,

'although you are late. What is this ceremony? I expected
to be fêted here by feasting, by food and flagons of wine.
Why bring me weapons when I wish for a young virgin?
Why bring me such faces as yours, wearing mirthless
expressions?'

'We come to kill you, Father,' said Aledref.

'Our weapons are for death, not celebration,' said
Cedred.

'But first we will hear what you have to say,' said
Woundrel.

'Say? I've nothing to say!' roared Harmon. 'Don't you
dare speak of killing! I've always been a good father to
you. And to the girls. Fed you. Wiped your dirty little bottoms when you were babies. Carried you on my back
when you were toddlers. Let you swarm all over me.
Taught you how to run, how to fight. Told you stories of
my own youth, how I killed that dragon.'

Cedred said, 'Ah, you never killed no dragon. You made
that up.'

'Son, you don't know what naked courage means. By
Jarl, what a life you led me, what a damned nuisance you
were! Spoiling my sleep, ruining my siestas, wrecking my
love life. Even when I had managed to get your mother
down on her back and—'

'We don't want to hear,' shouted Aledref.

Harmon pointed a quivering finger at him. 'Oh, you can
smirk, Aledref, but you were the worst. A stupid, arrogant kid! Yet I sacrificed years to your welfare.'

Aledref spoke with chill in his voice. 'Our complaint is
not with what you did or did not do, Father, but with
what you are.'

'Oh? And what am I exactly, in your thick-headed
estimation?'

Cedred answered, his voice as cold as his elder brother's. 'You are a nonentity, Father. That's what we most resent. That's why we are about to kill you.'

'Me? A nonentity? Why you fool, I'm the source of your life. I'm known all about for my martial skills. Do I not laugh, weep, bleed, pee with some force and splendour, and many other things? A non— What? I never heard such nonsense. I wouldn't think you three added up to much, either! Didn't I invent that flying machine?'

'It crashed, Father,' said Aledref.

'Only because you did not flap the wings rapidly enough.'

'That's enough talk, Father,' Cedred said, glancing at Aledref for approval. 'You're full of bluster as usual. Now it's time to kill you.'

Woundrel intervened, saying, 'Let Father make a last sacrifice to the Sun God before he dies.'

'Bugger the Sun God,' roared Harmon. 'I'll knock your blocks off with my staff if you dare come near me.' Turning to his daughters, Via, Roa and Day, he said, 'What do you think your poor dead mother would say if she could hear these impertinences, girls?'

Via laughed. 'Oh, she'd say "Like father, like sons", I imagine.'

'You've always made light of things, you little bitch,' said Harmon. He turned to Roa. 'Have you got a good word for me, Roa, dear? You know how I've always loved you the best of the lot.'

'Really, Dad? Yet you forgot my birthdays. You were always away when I wanted you, wouldn't come near me when I was ill . . .'

'You were always a sickly little creature.'

'Sickly? I was undernourished. You have always given

precedence to these three greedy pigs of boys, made me wait on them and clean up after them, although it must have been obvious even to you that I was far more intelligent than they were. Who was it who first thought of cooking and flavouring meat with herbs? Why, *me*, of course!'

'Mother had the idea for the herbs,' said Day, quietly, and congratulated herself for having slipped in the remark.

'Mother!' exclaimed Roa with disgust. 'Mother – what did she ever do? A useless bit of goods. Personally, Father, I think you chose to mate with her because she was so *stupid* . . . You really really needed someone who was more stupid than you. No wonder your sons turned out to be such morons.'

'Look who's talking!' exclaimed Aledref. 'Who accidentally sat on a python? Who invented dresses? Who fell in the stream and had to be rescued when she was a girl?'

Roa retorted angrily, 'I fell in because you deliberately let go of my hand as I was leaning over the river bank. And what was I doing? Trying to teach you how to tickle a trout! But no, you and those stupid, moronic brothers of yours could not learn the art, just as you've never learnt to fish with a line. As for—'

'Stop it!' roared Harmon. 'Shut up this instant, all of you! You're always bickering. You always bickered. You always will bicker. You're all a pain in my neck. Between you, you've made my life miserable. I've never married again because you lot were always around.'

So the argument continued. The Sun God rose, pale and etiolated, while the family brought up old grudges and rehearsed them. Once silence fell, when the children of Harmon lay in the damp grass, trying to remember other older grievances.

Harmon it was who, leaning on his staff, arose, sighing deeply and brushing dirt from his robe.

'Well, old as I am, I'm off. I'm going to leave you to your own devices. I'm going to enjoy a real life in my declining years.'

Aledref picked up the axe which had lain at his feet throughout the morning. 'You don't escape from us that easily, Father. You'd always be hanging about somewhere, trying to mess up our lives. Not no more! Are you ready, boys?'

Woundrel held up a hand. 'No, let's not be too hasty, Aledref. I mean, when you think of it, there's something in what Father says about our always bickering. I wondered—'

'But we're not always bickering,' Cedred exclaimed. 'You're the one who bickers. When did I bicker? I always keep my trap shut, otherwise Aledref hits me.'

'I haven't hit you for years!'

'But you are a bit of a thug, let's face it.'

'I'm not. I'm your protector. Who fought off that baboon last week?'

'I was trying to make a pet of it.'

'Oh, Jarl! You two creeps!' exclaimed Woundrel, breaking into this dialogue. 'Roa is right. We certainly behave like morons. Roa is more intelligent – and certainly nicer looking.'

Roa blew Woundrel a kiss. 'Come to bed with me again tonight, my darling brother!' she called.

'Right, that's enough!' said Harmon. 'I declare the meeting closed. It's getting near lunchtime. Let's go. Via, prepare us something simple. Don't go to too much trouble. No more of that iguana with larks thrust down its throat. And let's all have a pleasant afternoon. You could go down by the river bank, with no bickering, all friendly together.'

At his words, Aledref immediately seized his axe, and Cedred his dagger. 'You don't get away like that. We're going to kill you, you nonentity! Right now!'

Via jumped forward, waving her hands in distress. She stood in front of her father, confronting her brothers. 'Wait! I know perhaps Father deserves to be killed for all the awful things he has done, and for the good things he failed to do – like, at least in my case, educating me. But you might have the goodness to kill him honestly. Forget all this nonentity business. We're all nonentities. Oh yes, we are, Aledref – or else why would we still be living in this miserable forest? Why have I got no decent flowers to stick in my hair?'

'We are a bit primitive,' said Day, laughing nervously. The others ignored her.

'Jarl, how the girl goes on!' exclaimed Aledref, sneering at Via. 'Get out of the way, darling, or you may be killed too.'

'If you wish to come back into my bed tonight, you had better listen to what I have to say,' Via told him.

Flaunting her hips, she walked over to her father, and put an arm condescendingly on his shoulder. 'Father, these silly boys are unable to tell you why they are about to kill you; their powers of analysis are limited. So *I* will tell you. The truth is that whatever they do, they feel themselves stifled by your presence. They can't have a mature life until you have gone. You may or may not be a nonentity, but it is your life, your being on Earth, which stifles their existence.'

Harmon had cowered on his improvised throne before his sons' threats. Now he had collected himself. He answered his daughter calmly, in a quiet voice. 'No, that is not the truth of the matter. I do not stifle their lives. This "feeling stifled" is an expression of their own inadequacy. It has little to do with me. In fact I am their hope, your hope — Aledref's, Cedred's, Woundrel's, Roa's, Day's and yours, my dear good Via. Because when I am transfixed by the Sun God's arrows, when I am gone from this world into the arms of the Sun God, then you will find that his gaze will be fixed on you. You will be the next generation to depart. As long as I am here, walking about, boozing, sweating, chasing women, swearing, shitting — whatever it is you most dislike about me — you can feel safe. Once I'm gone — well, those golden arrows will be aimed at your miserable selfish hearts.'

A silence fell as his words sunk in. Even Aledref turned his fierce gaze to the ground, as he attempted to think. It was as if he already felt that golden bow drawn and that arrow which brought death turned in the direction of his vitals.

Day gathered courage to speak. 'We can't just kill Pa just like that. There has to be a proper trial. Besides, what would Mother think of us? You know, it's possible she is watching us from — well, just from another sphere. Maybe she is looking down on us even now . . . I have a theory that she simply turned into a deer and just ran off into the forest.'

Roa laughed scornfully. 'Turned into a hippo, more like!'

But Day would not be deflected. She told them that there was a spiritual aspect to all of what she called 'the silly talk of killing'. She told them that they must realise that their father, if just murdered, might become an even worse threat to their well-being and his ghost return to haunt them. Maybe the ghost, she said, would poison the water hole, or infest just the hut with cockroaches.

Woundrel told her loftily that cockroaches had yet to evolve. The things crawling about were trilobites. He stamped on one as it went past.

It seemed to Day that there were certain conditions here she might easily improve. While they were on the subject of housing, she said, it was just very unhealthy to have a wood fire in the middle of the hut. It was smoky and smoking was bad for them. She rounded on her brothers, asking them why they just did not build a stove and a chimney, instead of lying around all day.

'We're tired,' said Cedred. 'It's the malnutrition.'

'I can't quite visualise a chimney,' said Woundrel.

'I'm thinking of getting married,' said Aledref.

Harmon was thoughtfully regarding his toes. 'I have never married again. You lot were always hanging around with your miserable disparaging remarks. Bickering, always bickering. Now I'm going to leave you to your own devices. My declining years are to be spent in real independence.'

'Oh dear, oh golly gosh!' exclaimed Day. 'Are you always so cruel to each other? It makes the twenty-second century seem just nice. How do I get back there, I wonder?'

Via clouted her for talking nonsense. Day burst into tears, which served to make the others laugh.

'Well, I've had my say. Now I'm off,' said Harmon, with a sigh, as he rose from his seat.

Aledref barred his way. He said that as long as his father was alive, he would always be somewhere in the neighbourhood, making them feel inferior. He turned to his brothers, to run a finger suggestively across his throat.

Woundrel told him to wait, claiming that there was, after all, something in what their father said about them always bickering.

Cedred denied they were always bickering. 'In any case, you're the one who bickers.'

'When did I ever bicker?' Woundrel asked, angrily. 'If I don't keep my trap shut, Aledref hits me.'

Aledref denied it. He had not hit Woundrel in years. Cedred told him that nevertheless he was a thug.

Aledref denied that too. Had he not been Cedred's protector? He had fought off the baboon attacking Cedred only a week ago.

'You scared it off, yes,' said Cedred. 'But I was trying to make a pet of it. You're always interfering in my life.'

Woundrel was lying on his back, trying to make a daisy chain with his feet and toes. He glanced scornfully at his brothers. 'You two creeps are always yakking on. Roa was right when she said we were morons. We certainly behave like morons. Roa is much more intelligent than we will ever be. Besides which, she smells nicer and is nicer looking.'

Roa blew Woundrel a kiss and invited him to come into her bed again at nightfall.

'Didn't we go through all this before?' asked Day, uneasily. Their memories seemed alarmingly short.

Harmon clapped his hands and declared the meeting closed. Turning to Day, he ordered her to go and prepare the sort of delicacy he had been hoping for, such as baked lizard with thrushes stuffed down its throat. Day recoiled at the mere suggestion. She blew her nose on a leaf.

As Harmon rose, shifting uneasily from one foot to the other, Aledref picked up his axe and Cedred his dagger. They advanced on their father, calling him a nonentity and saying they were about to strike. Via moved protectively in front of him.

'Wait!' she said. 'I know Father deserves all he gets. Not only for the bad things he has done but for the good things he failed to do, such as not teaching me astronomy or giving me an education. I've no idea what twice two could be! But after all, we are nonentities ourselves, the very dregs of evolution.'

'Oh, that's just not true,' Day interposed. 'At least, I don't think it's true. I'd guess you are *homo erectus*. Perhaps that was a blind just alley . . .'

'Don't talk rubbish,' said Aledref, pushing her aside. 'I don't know about you girls but I've evolved from an ape, a higher ape. Out of the way, kids, or you'll get yourselves killed.'

Via kicked him in the shin. 'You'd better listen to me if you want to come into my bed tonight. So shut up!' She turned to her father, doing creepy movements, with hands outspread on either side of her head, to hold his attention.

'Father, these stupid boys of yours dare not let on about the real reasons why they want to kill you, so I will tell you. The truth is, they feel stifled by your presence. They feel they can't lead a mature life until you are dead and gone.'

The words made Harmon explode. Seldom had he heard such nonsense, he said. He had never tried to stifle anyone – whereas his own father had always tried to stifle him. They were just inadequate, that was the truth, and were looking for excuses. In fact, he was their only hope – their one and only hope.

'What?' Day exclaimed. 'Doesn't religion come into the picture? You must have some religion, surely.'

Harmon ordered her to keep the Sun God out of the argument.

'Now I'm off,' he said, making to go.

'No, please wait, Father,' said Woundrel, coming forward, laying a hand on his father's arm. 'I don't see this matter quite as Via does. There's some truth in what she says, but she's only a girl, and things are easier for girls.'

'Don't you believe it!' shrieked Roa. 'Pig!'

But Woundrel was not to be deflected, and continued to speak in a quiet voice. 'You see, as long as you are still swaggering about, well, Aledref and Cedred and I don't – well, we're just *sons*. I mean, we are no more than sons.'

'You're *my* sons!' the old man said, proudly.

'That's the problem. We want to be men, not sons.'

'You are men. Pretty feeble men . . . What are you talking about?' Harmon glared at his son. 'Why has no one invented psychiatry?'

'What I am trying to say is that we shall feel ourselves to be real men only when you have gone from the Earth. Killing you is necessary for us to live as men, free, mature, in control of our own destinies . . .'

'In other words, killing you is a sort of initiation rite,' explained Aledref. 'Like this!' Raising the axe above his head, he brought the blade down on his father's shoulder, close to his left ear.

Harmon uttered a cry. He endeavoured to swing his staff, but Cedred rushed in and sank his dagger into his father's stomach. As Harmon fell backwards, his staff went flying through the air, to fall some feet away. Roa seized it, ran forward, and smashed it against her father's skull.

'Take that for all your wickedness!' she cried.

The three of them, Aledref, Cedred, and Roa, beat at

the old man as he rolled over on to his stomach. He attempted to rise, drawing himself to his knees, but they smashed him down again with axe, dagger and staff. They worked away, cursing and gasping, long after Harmon's soul had fled into the arms of the Sun God.

'Jarl, that's enough,' cried Aledref, exhausted. 'We're men now, the three of us!' After clasping Roa's and Cedred's hands, he sat down on his father's crumpled body and wiped the sweat from his brow.

'Don't sit there like that!' cried Roa. 'You'll get all bloody, and then who'll have to wash your loin-skirt?'

Coming forward, Woundrel appealed to Aledref. 'So, you've done the deed. At least let's have the decency to eat him now.'

'Forget it. What did he ever do for us?' Turning to his other brother and to Roa, Aledref clicked his fingers. He rose, pushing Woundrel aside.

Day was shrieking. 'Horror, horror!' she cried. 'And my family were Baptists just!'

They severed their father's head and his genitals, and buried them in the clearing. From his stomach they pulled out his intestines and threw the length of them into the forest.

Woundrel stood watching the proceedings in silence, pale of face.

Via burst into tears and ran from the clearing. That night, preparing their supper, eyes still blinded by tears, she accidentally plucked a poisonous herb with which to flavour the stew. They all became sick.

When the Sun God next spread his cloth of dawn over the world, all the children of Harmon were lifeless. But from the buried head of Harmon grew the Tree of Knowledge, and from his buried genitals two persons were created, a man and a woman. And from the intestines, lying in the forest, a serpent was created.

And the man and woman, innocent in their nakedness, looked on the world and found it good. At least until the serpent turned up.

And so a new myth was born.

HEADLESS

A vast crowd was gathering to see Flammerion behead himself. The TV people and Flammerion had rehearsed almost every move so that the event would go without a hitch. It was estimated that some 1.8 billion people would be watching: the largest TV audience since the nuking of North Korea.

Some people preferred to watch the event live. Seats in the stadium, highly priced, were booked months in advance.

Among the privileged were Alan Ibrox Kumar and his wife Dorothea Kumar, the Yakaphrenia Lady. They discussed it as they flew in to Dusseldorf.

'Why is he giving all the proceeds to Children of Turkmenistan, for heaven's sake?' Alan exclaimed.

'The terrible earthquake . . . Surely you remember?'

'I remember, yes, yes. But Flammerion's European, isn't he?'

For answer, she said, 'Get me another gin, will you?' She had yet to reveal to him she was divorcing him directly after the beheading.

The Swedish royal family had reserved two seats in a back row. They felt that Sweden should be represented at what was increasingly regarded – by the media at any rate – as an important event. The Swedish government remained furious that their offer of a prominent site in Stockholm had been turned down by Flammerion's agent.

Fortunately, six Swedes, two of them women, had since volunteered to behead themselves, either in Stockholm or preferably Uppsala. They named the charities they preferred.

Dr Eva Berger had booked a seat in the stadium on the day the box office opened. She had counselled Flammerion, advising against his drastic action on health grounds. When she realised she was unable to deflect him from his purpose, she begged him that at least a percentage of the proceeds go towards the Institute of Psychoanalysts. Flammerion had replied, 'I am offering you my psychiatric example. What else do you want? Don't be greedy.'

Later, Dr Berger had sold her seat for nineteen times the amount she had paid for it. She felt her integrity had paid off.

Dr Berger's feckless nephew, Leigh, happened to be a cleaner in the Düsseldorf stadium. 'Thank God I'm not on duty tonight,' he said. 'There'll be one hell of a mess. Blood everywhere.'

'That's what the public pay for,' said his boss. 'Blood has a whole vast symbolism behind it. It's not just a red liquid, son. You've heard of bad blood, and princes of the blood, and blood boiling, or things done in cold blood, haven't you? We've got a whole mythology on our hands, no less, tonight. And I need you to do an extra shift.'

Leigh looked hang-dog and asked what they would do with the head when Flammerion had finished with it.

His boss told him it would be auctioned at Sotheby's in London.

Among those who were making money from the event was Cynthia Saladin. She had sold her story to the media worldwide. Most people on the globe were conversant with what Cynthia and Flammerion had done in bed. Cynthia had tried her best to entertain, and was now married to a Japanese businessman. Her book, 'Did Circumcision Start Flammy Going Funny?' had been rushed into print, and was available everywhere.

Flammerion was passably good-looking. Commentators remarked on the numbers of ugly men who had bought seats in the stadium. Among their numbers was Monty Wilding, the British film director whose face had been likened to a wrinkled plastic bag. Monty was boasting that his exploitation flick, *Trouble Ahead* was already at the editing stage.

The Green Party protested against the movie, and about the self-execution, claiming that it was worse than a blood-sport and would undoubtedly start a trend. British sportsmen, too, were up in arms. The beheading clashed with the evening of the Cup Final. F.A IN HEAD-OFF COLLISION, ran the headlines in the *Sun*.

There were others in Britain equally incensed by what was taking place on the continent. Among them were those who remained totally ignorant of the whereabouts of Turkmenistan.

As so often in times of trouble, people turned towards their solicitors, the Archbishop of Canterbury and Gore Vidal for consolation – not necessarily in that order.

The Archbishop delivered a fine sermon on the subject,

reminding the congregation that Jesus had given His life that we might live, and that that 'we' included the common people of England as well as the Tory party. Now here was another young man, Borgo Flammerion, prepared to give up his life for the suffering children of Central Asia – if that indeed was where Turkmenistan was situated.

It was true, the Archbishop continued, that Christ had not permitted Himself to be crucified before the television cameras, but that was merely an unfortunate accident of timing. The few witnesses of the Crucifixion whose words had come down to us were notoriously unreliable. Indeed, it was possible (as much must be readily admitted) that the whole thing was a cock-and-bull story. Had Christ postponed the event by a millennium or two, photography would have provided a reliable testament to His self-sacrifice, and then perhaps everyone in Britain would believe in Him, instead of just a lousy nine per cent.

Meanwhile, the Archbishop concluded, we should all pray for Flammerion, that the deed he contemplated be achieved without pain.

Visibly put out by this address, the British Prime Minister made an acid retort in the House of Commons on the following day. She said, amid general laughter, that at least *she* was not losing her head. 'My head is not for turning,' she stated, amid laughter.

She added that the Archbishop of Canterbury should ignore what went on in Europe and look to her own parish. Why, a murder had taken place in Canterbury just the previous month. Whatever might or might not be happening in Düsseldorf, one thing was certain: Great Britain was pulling out of recession.

This much-applauded speech was delivered only hours before Flammerion performed in public.

As the stadium began to fill, bands played solemn music and old Beatles' hits. Coachloads of French people of all sexes arrived. The French took particular interest in *L'Événement Flammerion*, claiming the performer to be of French descent, although born in St Petersburg of a Russian mother. This statement had irritated elements of the American press, who pointed out that there was a St Petersburg in Florida, too.

A belated move was afoot to have Flammerion extradited to Florida, to be legally executed for Intended Suicide, now a capital offence.

The French, undeterred, filled the press with long articles of analysis, under such headings as FLAMMY: EST IL PÉDALE? T-shirts, depicting the hero with head and penis missing, were selling well.

The country which gained most from the event was Germany. Already a soap was running on TV called *Kopf Kaput*, about an amusing Bavarian family, all of whom were busy buying chainsaws with which to behead each other. Some viewers read a political message into *Kopf Kaput*.

Both the Red Cross and the Green Crescent paraded round the stadium. They had already benefited enormously from the publicity. The Green Crescent ambulances were followed by lorries on which lay young Turkmen victims of the earthquake in blood-stained bandages. They were cheered to the echo. All told, a festival air prevailed.

Behind the scenes, matters were almost as noisy. Gangs of well-wishers and autograph hunters queued for a sight of their hero. In another bunch stood professional men and women who hoped, even at this late hour, to dissuade Flammerion from his fatal act. Any number of objections to the act were raised. Among these objections were the moral repulsiveness of the act itself, its effect on children, the fact that Cynthia still loved her man, the fear of a riot should Flammerion's blade miss its mark, and the question whether the act was possible as Flammerion proposed it. Among the agitated objectors were cutlers, eager to offer a sharper blade.

None of these people, no priests, no sensation-seekers, no surgeons offering to replace the head immediately it was severed, were allowed into Flammerion's guarded quarters.

Borgo Flammerion sat in an office chair, reading a copy of the Russian *Poultry Dealer's Monthly*. As a teenager, he had lived on a poultry farm. Earning promotion, he had worked for a while in the slaughterhouse before emigrating to Holland, where he had robbed a patisserie. Later, he was lead singer with a group, The Sluice Gates.

He was dressed now in a gold lamé blouson jacket, sable tights and lace-up boots. His head was shaven; he had taken advice on this.

On the table before him lay a brand new cleaver, especially sharpened by a man from Geneva, a representative of the Swiss company that had manufactured the instrument. Flammerion glanced at this cleaver every so often, as he read about a startling new method of egg-retrieval. Figures on his digital watch writhed towards the hour of eight.

Behind him stood a nun, Sister Madonna, his sole companion in these last days. She was chosen because she had once made a mistaken pilgrimage to Ashkhabad, capital of Turkmenistan, believing she was travelling to Allahabad in India.

At a signal from the sister, Flammerion closed his periodical. Rising, he took up the cleaver. He walked up the stairs with firm tread, to emerge into the dazzle of floodlights.

An American TV announcer dressed in a blood-red gown said sweetly, 'If your immediate viewing plans do not include decapitation this evening, may we advise you to look away for a few minutes.'

When the applause died, Flammerion took up a position between the chalk marks.

He bowed without smiling. When he whirled the cleaver to his right side, the blade glittered in the lights. The crowd fell silent as death.

Flammerion brought the blade up sharply, so that it sliced from throat to nape-of-neck. His head fell cleanly away from his body.

He remained standing for a moment, letting the cleaver drop from his grasp.

The stadium audience was slow to applaud. But all had gone exceptionally well, considering that Flammerion had had no proper dress rehearsal.

BEEF

'Thank goodness, the cow is now extinct!' said Coriander Avorry, in the final year of this millennium.

Avorry was speaking at the Peterborough Ecological Crisis Management Conference, late last century. He had recently assumed the presidency of the ECM Association. Although his announcement roused a deal of applause, there were many delegates who thought that the final extinction of the cow – and of ninety-nine per cent of the world's sheep – had come about too late.

'For too long,' Avorry continued, 'motives of profit and high yield dominated agriculture. Biotech took over compassion. Industrial agricultural practice has slowly broken the so-called developing, actually decaying, nations. Now our greed has brought the First World to disaster.'

It was then that the bomb exploded. It had been planted under the dais. Many in the hall were injured, some fatally, including Avorry.

His daughter, herself slightly wounded, ran to his aid. She threw herself down by his side, weeping to see his terrible injuries.

Who planted the bomb? It could have been the Meat-Eaters on the one hand or, on the other, the Undead.

Consider their cases dispassionately, if possible. The Undead had as their objective the ruination of the First World. Fortress Europe had previously been breached with the aid of H-bombs manufactured in India and Pakistan. Although the Undead were a comparatively small unit, their fanaticism knew no reason or compromise. They were perennially reinforced by members of the Third World.

Although Third World debts had been rescinded and placatory loans paid over, 'ransom money!' cried the throats of Africa. The Undead came from a dislocated world. There, literally billions of people lived and suffered on starvation's edge. They were landless. Powerful companies had bought up the land, farming it – raping it – with fertilisers and pesticides and inappropriate monocultures. So the landless and uprooted could obtain food only by payment. And when they could no longer pay – well, the improvidence of the poor was well-known. They died of it, unwanted and unwashed.

And where did the food grown on their land go?

Take India. According to the Undead's campaign statistics, forty per cent of arable land was devoted to growing fodder for animals which were killed and exported. Other acreage grew soya beans – exported to feed the cattle of the First World. The old India, frugal as it was, had died. Its poor farmers had once relied on cattle for dung and for pulling and carrying-power. Now prices had soared beyond their reach. Such farmers and their families were now dead – or building bombs.

Such was the background of most of the Undead.

Now consider the case of the Meat-Eaters. Their claim

was that if they ceased to market beef, the entire world economy would collapse. At this time, this claim had a grain of truth in it, since collapse was imminent in any case.

The Meat-Eaters' anodyne picture of the world depicted cattle grazing placidly on green pastures. This had become fantasy long before the end. The truth was that sentient creatures – not only cattle, but sheep, pigs and fowls – were no longer animals but mere meat-production units, destined to make the journey into the greedy stomachs of the West as quickly and cheaply as possible.

To keep these meat-production units healthy in their short lives, they were stuffed with penicillin. So antibiotics became increasingly ineffectual in the task of curing an increasingly sick population. Their meat-gorging habits accelerated the rate of illness.

So the Meat-Eaters, as dedicatedly as the Undead in their different way, set the stage for global disaster.

What finally tipped the balance? The threat posed by the incursions of the Undead had caused the rural populations of Europe to withdraw to increasingly policed cities. In the neglected forests and woods, wild boar multiplied. Their numbers were estimated at two to three million in France, Germany, and Poland alone. Cases of CSF – Classical Swine Fever – were frequent, and spread to domesticated pigs. A stage of thought had been reached whereby it seemed indecent that any animal should roam unchecked in the wilds.

The German and French governments took it upon themselves to develop a genetically controlled virus which was unleashed on wild herds as, a century earlier, myxomatosis had been spread among rabbit populations. Biotech-shy neighbouring governments protested, to no avail.

Wild boar died in their thousands and hundreds of thousands. Their dead bodies lay in forests, copses and fields. The virus mutated and infected sheep. And from sheep a trans-specific variant spread to human beings.

Not since the Black Death had such devastation befallen the human race. Their dogs and cats, as well as their livestock, died with them. Their over-populated cities made ideal breeding grounds.

The Third World had its moment of triumph before it too was hit. Amongst the undernourished populations, CSF spread rapidly.

The world economy collapsed, crumbling like an old man without teeth.

Such survivors as there were had to make do in a different world. It was an even harsher world than the one preceding it. But one thing was certain: all men were now perforce vegetarians. Their cattle had been wiped out.

Coriander Avorry had been a vegetarian all along.

So who was responsible for his death? The Meat-Eaters, busy trying to re-establish the old order? Or the Undead, busy trying to destroy the remnants of Western civilisation?

The world was too chaotic for the crime to be solved.

One thing was certain, as his weeping daughter declared. Avorry was dead.

So were the cows.

Meat Makes You Ill. It Has Made the Whole Planet Ill.

NOTHING IN LIFE
IS EVER ENOUGH

My life has carried strange echoes of an old play. It was early one morning towards the end of winter when I first set foot on that magical island — that magical island where I loved before I knew love's name. The sun, rising late, dazzled my eyes and cast gaunt shadows towards me. I walked through a maze of alternating sunlight and shade as I made my way along a path among trees, leading up from the little stone harbour to the one unruined house on the island, a house or castle perched on an eminence, yet protected from the north winds by a slightly greater eminence which hunched its shoulder above the ragged rooftops and towers of the house.

As I went, a sound rose above the splash of waves breaking against the shore. A few steps more and then I halted, listening. A young woman was walking by the house, singing, singing to please herself. And how it pleased me! Her figure moved in and out of shadow. That was my first sight of Miranda, and my first time of listening to her lovely voice.

A strange prickling of the skin attended my approach to her. Conflicting premonitions filled my mind. Was I to encounter a strange enchantment, or was I in fact coming home?

In the final year of the nineteen-sixties, life was quite different from what it is now. I dropped out of school and left my parents. I was what was later to be called a hippie. My intention, however, was to live my own life by myself, as far as that was possible. I thought I might become a poet.

My wanderings took me far from home. Eventually, I found myself in the north of the country, in an area where there is little habitation. There I fell ill. A man and wife who ran a small restaurant looked after me until I was well. His name was Ferdinand Robson, hers Roberta.

These two seemingly good-natured people told me they had also escaped from a life with which they had no sympathy, the life of the industrial towns. However, when I saw how hard they worked to keep their restaurant going, and the small guest house that went with it, I thought they had delivered themselves into another form of servitude.

Robson seemed to think as much. His air of melancholy suggested it. He advised me to go to the coast, where there was an off-shore island. He suggested I might get some casual work there.

Who lived on the island? I asked.

He answered abruptly: Only an author. Otherwise, no one.

He turned away with a black expression on his face.

I cannot think why this information, that look, so troubled me.

As I was putting together my few possessions to leave, Roberta came to my room, with her round face and her angry look. She said that her husband was upset; he owed me some explanation for his abrupt behaviour. I protested, but she ignored me. This is what she said, staring at me with her dark haunted eyes.

'Never gamble, young lad. Not with your possessions. Not with your money. Not with people. Not with your soul. You understand?'

My reply was that no, I did not understand. How could you gamble with other people, I asked.

'If you are mad enough, you can gamble with their lives. There's no recklessness, no wickedness, like it. Can you comprehend that, lad?'

Although I muttered that I did comprehend, I comprehended neither her meaning nor the intensity with which she spoke.

After a moment's silence, she seemed to control herself. When she spoke again, her manner was calmer.

'How you will fare on that island remains to be seen You are young. Perhaps you do not yet understand that when we take one path through life, we must abandon others. Those other paths will never be open to us again. Later, we may regret the path we chose, but it is impossible to retrace our steps. To attempt to do so spells disaster.'

I was puzzled by this statement. Perhaps I truly was, as she said, too young then to understand. I asked if she spoke of love.

'Not only love but many other elements which comprise life.' She thought for a while, then went on impetuously, 'Ferdinand, my husband, was once extremely rich. He made his money as a speculator in the City. He was reckless. He contracted a mistaken marriage, in which his then wife bore a son – a son who grew into a wicked deceitful boy. When Ferdinand and I met, he sought to change his life and his lifestyle. His divorce cost him dear. His business deals collapsed. He owned the island to which you are going.'

'I see,' I said.

'No, you don't see.' She turned away from me, and leaned on the window sill to stare out at the empty countryside. 'In the end, he had to sell the island to buy this place – to which we are now chained. In truth, he gambled his wealth away, the imbecile. He has hopes that we can make enough money to buy back what he still believes is his island. It is beautiful – though whether we would be happy there is another question . . . He hopes we may live there before we are too old.'

'And your hopes, Mrs Robson?'

She stared hard at me. I saw she thought the gulf between our experiences was too great to bridge by any confidence. 'Never mind *my* hopes,' she said. 'Off you go to yours.'

She patted my cheek.

When I arrived in the early morning on the island, the eastern sky was still barred with red and gold cloud. Miranda had been milking a goat. She carried a pail of milk. As I approached, she stood stock still, clutching the pail. She spoke little, hardly replying to my greeting, and led me by a back way into the kitchens. So I entered Prosperity House – as it was ambitiously called. There were few signs of prosperity or modernity. Among other tenants, monks had occupied the castle in the seventeenth century, and had built on a small chapel, now unused.

The girl – I found it hard to judge her age, but reckoned she was still a child – led me to her father, through corridors where most of the windows were shuttered; only at one window was the sunshine allowed to break in, to spread mystery rather than light throughout the long corridor. At a far door, Miranda knocked timidly on its worn panels. A muffled voice bid us enter.

She pushed me in ahead of her.

I entered the sanctum sanctorum of Prosperity House, a vast dull room, the walls of which, hung with tapestries of various design, made it seem vaster and yet stifling. In one corner of this room was a large desk, at which sat a large heavy man, bearded and past middle age. A stack of untidy paper lay before him. He uttered no greeting, but sat and regarded me with a remarkable lack of interest.

His daughter, likewise, wasted no time on courtesies, but went to a heavy fabric and dragged it back to reveal a north-facing window. The light entering, rather than mitigating the suffocating darkness of the room, made the desk lamp seem to burn more dimly.

Advancing to the desk, I announced myself, saying I had come to work as casual labour on the island.

The large man rose, leaned over the desk and extended a large hand, which I shook rather tentatively. 'Eric Magistone,' he said, in a deep voice.

He contemplated me from under his eyebrows before saying that his daughter would show me my duties. Then he slumped back in his chair.

Miranda seemed rather perplexed about what I should do. 'You could chop some wood for a start,' she said.

I did as I was told. It was strange taking orders from a child, though a beautiful one, particularly since I was not long past childhood myself.

The house had once been a castle, built to defend the coast from marauding nations, the Danes in particular. Its previous owner, Ferdinand Robson, had extended it, throwing out a wing and a conservatory. A shutter, blown off in a violent storm some years ago, had shattered the glass of the conservatory roof. The conservatory was in consequence shut off, given over to decay. I was installed in a room in the tower, where I slept.

Work was not arduous. Once a week, a small boat came over from the mainland to deliver supplies. On me devolved the business of taking down to the harbour money in payment, and lugging the box of supplies back to the house. I also took over the milking of the goat, and searched for the eggs the hens laid near or sometimes in the house.

I took to roving the island when not actively employed. To the south was a small pool or corrie, in which I could swim. I found many other delights. The monks, when the building had served as a monastery, had planted orchards, which still survived. Later owners had attempted a vegetable garden. Here and there, in unexpected nooks, grew fruit bushes, as well as nut and fruit trees, their seeds presumably dropped by birds, with which the island was well-stocked; birds seemed to call from every tree. As well as birds of flight, there were pheasants, partridges, and some peacocks, which pierced the night with their cries. Wild cats also flourished, and rabbits by the score.

The island became my delight. It was the paradise I always hoped to find, yet never expected to come upon. It was particularly rich in small wild plants, of which I learned the names from a book in the library. I took delight in naming the poor man's weather glass, which came into flower in May, the white dead-nettle, with its heart-shaped leaves, the beautiful and invasive Japanese knotweed, beneath whose tall bamboo-like stems sheltered lily-of-the-valley, with its sweet scent, the bush vetch and greater celandine, the pretty white bryony which carries red berries in season. Many more. Ferns too, and tall daisies with small imitation suns at their hearts.

I came on a sheltered place where stood a ruinous hut, almost entirely hidden by bramble. This I called Paradise Gully. Here I would lie for hours on end when not called upon to work, reading books I found in the library, old-fashioned books: romances by Dumas and Jules Verne, novels by Thomas Hardy and Dostoevsky, and the plays of Shakespeare – one of which in particular took my fancy, since it was set on an island.

At the same time, I learned something about Eric Magistone from his daughter. He had been born Derek Stone, of modestly wealthy parents who, from an early age, had encouraged his love of learning. Although he went into the family business, his ambition was to become a writer. At the age of twenty-one, he published his first book, *A Pain in the Necromancer*. It was a comic novel which sold extremely well. He followed it with more of the same, *Getting it in the Necromancer*.

And then the first novel was bought by Hollywood.

I protested when I learned this history, piece by piece, from Miranda. Could it be that that grim and solitary man, who rarely left his study, wrote comic novels?

It was so – or had been so in his youth. But more than that. Eric Magistone (by this time his pen name had become his legal name) flew to Hollywood, where he wrote the screenplay of his novel. Even more, the film was a tremendous comedy success. Even more, it spawned a series of comic magical adventures, for all of which Magistone was well-paid to write the screenplays. He became fashionable, and a favourite with the ladies. From one of those liaisons, his daughter Miranda was born.

The event changed his way of life. He bought the island, I was told, from Ferdinand Robson, whose financial affairs were in disarray, and came to live here with his mistress and their daughter. Life on the island, after the glitter of Hollywood, did not suit the mistress; one fine morning, Magistone woke and found her gone, leaving behind not only a daughter but an ill-spelt letter of farewells and pathetic excuses.

'Is he still writing his comedies?' I asked Miranda.

She shook her pretty black curls. 'He is writing a huge book, very serious, very long, very deep, which will explain everything in the world.' She stretched out her arms to show me how big everything was.

I was taken with this idea. There was much that needed explanation. Now I could understand why Magistone was so stern and solitary; he had undertaken a grave responsibility.

'Will he explain about the Moon? Will he explain why water freezes? Will he explain why we see colours? Will he speak about the various seasons? Will he tell us why we die? Will he say why boys and girls are different?'

Such questions we discussed together, Miranda and I, in Paradise Gully, huddling together when the spring days turned chill.

I had discovered that Miranda had never explored the island on which she lived. Indeed, she barely went out of the house, except to visit the goat shed. Her father had forbidden her access to the island, on the grounds that unknown dangers lurked there. She was at first terrified, but I clutched her hand and lured her on. To my and her intense delight, I was able to unfold for her the beauties of the island, the patches of gorse, the beds of heather, the cherry trees in flower, the daffodils that shook their heads in the breeze, the primroses that spread their bright and humble petals nearly to the southern shore, all the pleasing and modest details of nature, and the flowers of summer, as summer came in with its bumble bees and sweet smells.

I taught her a skill I had only recently learned, of fishing for fish in the corrie. These captives we cooked over a wood fire we built in the Gully, to eat them by the light of the flames as evening closed upon us.

We were spontaneous together, this beloved girl and I. We kissed each other out of happiness, and with no other thought. The fresh air changed her countenance from pale to ruddy, and she grew. She was as agile among the rocks as I. In the bay on the southern side of the island, we trawled the shallow water for shrimps, which we later boiled in a can and ate. No one supervised us. No one told us what to do or what not to do.

One evening, when we lazed upon the little beach, having dined on shrimps and crabs, we took off our clothes and swam in the warm sea. We splashed and laughed. When we emerged, we became solemn, gazing, marvelling, at each other's body, made ruddy by the setting sun. I ventured my finger into her little crack, above which a few dark hairs had begun to sprout. She touched and then held my little winkle, which responded readily to her grasp. Then we kissed with some knowledge in the kisses. My tongue found the sweet ribbed roof of her mouth.

It would be too easy to say that it was then we had fallen in love. We had no word for how we felt about each other. And I believe that I had always loved her, since I had first come upon her, standing in shadow with the pail of goat's milk held protectively in front of her.

We were then always in each other's company, and made love frequently, as fancy took us. I taught her how to catch rabbits and skin them, and how to tame a cat, which we called Abigail. Abigail, fed regularly on a diet of fish and rabbit, followed us everywhere like a dog, but would not enter the house. At the door, it arched its back and hissed in fright.

These were the days and weeks, even months, of our happiness. Miranda could read after a fashion. I often read to her, or we read together. We cried together over Alain-Fournier's lovely book: for we well understood that our happiness existed perilously in a world of misfortune and sorrow. Sun or Moon, we were together, interrupted only by occasional demands from her overbearing father.

In particular, I taught her to appreciate the music of Shakespeare's island story, on which there lives another Miranda. We likened me to a sort of Caliban and her father to a sort of Prospero, while our island was, of course, that magical island in the still-vexed Bermoothes.

Did time pass? I suppose it did. The Lord of the Island continued to write his great treatise on the improvement of mankind, while his daughter and I continued to live our lives as free spirits, enjoying – no, no, being part of – nature. Living our magical lives on the island.

There came the time when the silence of our nights was broken. A noise awoke me. I lay in Miranda's arms – for now we would not be separated even by sleep – and disentangled myself. I went to the window and stared out. The rain which had fallen earlier had blown away elsewhere. I looked down from my tower window upon the Moon reflected in a puddle on a worn flagstone.

Its pure image was broken by tramping feet.

Hammering sounded at a door far below. Miranda jumped up on the bed in a fright. I kissed the scanty patch of damp hair on her mound of Venus, trying to calm her. But she could only repeat in a frenzy, 'Oh God, it is the morning of my thirteenth birthday! The morning of my thirteenth birthday!'

Dressing hurriedly, I descended the winding stair. Already a pre-dawn light was fading vague shapes back into the world. On the ground floor, lights flashed on and off. Eric Magistone stood there, immobile as a statue, throwing his giant shadow on the wall. Near him, pacing fretfully, were two rough men in reefer jackets, swinging torches and muttering to each other in tones of complaint. The great door stood wide to the outside world, letting in its chill breath.

'Fetch down my daughter,' said Magistone, on seeing me. 'These men are here for her.'

'Why? What has she done?'

'Fetch down my daughter, I tell you, boy!' This order delivered in a roar. I ran to obey.

On the upper landing I met her, dressed, her hair still uncombed, clutching a small canvas bag. In the half light, her face was pallid, even ghostly. Though she shed no tear, her expression was one of extreme anguish.

In a choking voice, she said, 'We must part for ever, my dearest love.'

Downstairs, the brutish father kissed her before handing her over to the two men. 'Come on, miss,' one said. 'The tide is running.'

Then, with a backward glance towards me, she was gone from the house, gone between the two men.

When I made to follow, Magistone grasped my arm. 'Whatever you two have been up to, you don't follow. She's gone from us now, curse it. Curse my folly.'

Only slowly did I come to understand that Miranda was the victim of complex history. At one time, Magistone and Robson had been friends. They were gambling men. They lived together when Magistone was back from California, and shared the woman whom Roberta Robson had described as Ferdinand's first wife. Roberta had told me lies, as, it seemed, they all did, profound adult lies. The son born to this woman had been, not Robson's but Magistone's. Nor had he been wicked and deceitful, as Roberta had claimed. With irony, he too was called Ferdinand. He was beaten and abused by the two men.

At last they came to a falling out. Eventually, financial ruin meant that Robson had had to give the island to Magistone, now his enemy, in order to pay his debts. He had, however, extracted from Magistone one vital condition: namely, that Magistone would hand over his daughter Miranda on her thirteenth birthday, to be married to his (as he claimed) unfortunate son Ferdinand the Second.

I had not met this younger Ferdinand during my brief stay with the Robsons. He was away, working in the nearest big town.

It could be said that Magistone acted honourably in fulfilling his side of the bargain and handing over his daughter. Yet he did not consider what misery this pact would cause her. What he undoubtedly did consider, relishing its irony, was that the marriage would be incestuous, with his daughter marrying his son.

Or was that also a lie? I could not determine that as,

night after night, until summer rotted away into autumn, I was forced to attend on Magistone, to provide him with some kind of company, as he talked while drinking himself into oblivion.

But I too had my secret. On that day when the men had taken Miranda to her fate, I had finally broken free of Magistone and had run down to the water's edge – in time to see Miranda – my Miranda! – carried away across the morning waves in a speedy boat.

That was the last I ever saw of her. Something inside me was shattered for ever. From a youth I became old. Without her fresh and pure body, my own body seemed to decay. How terrible is the learning of wisdom!

With my mainspring broken, I had no thought of leaving the island where our happiness had been lived out. By day, the sullen sodden hulk of Magistone – I glimpsed him through the window of his study – sat in the gloom, writing his unending, awful book. While I – I lay in Paradise Gully, rewriting Shakespeare's masterpiece to accommodate my grief.

Shakespeare had made a great mistake. Shakespeare had not understood. I say this of the great dramatist, and perhaps thereby invite scorn. But he who had said 'Ripeness is all' forgot his own words. Now I knew how his drama should have ended.

It is Caliban's story. The company of men who have been shipwrecked on the isle proceed to the shore, among them Ferdinand, Prince of Naples. Prospero has burnt his enormous impossible book and is also to leave the island. He takes with him his daughter Miranda, who must marry the foppish Ferdinand. She has no say in the matter. Marriage is what her father has decided upon.

They all gather on the shore, while sailors make ready the boat that will take them out to the galleon anchored in the bay. Soon Caliban will be alone on the island that is rightfully his.

And then – this the Bard did not foresee – Miranda slips her little hand from Ferdinand's and runs! Runs for her life! Hides in a gully in a great spread of knotweed. The soldiers search for her. But night comes on, the concealing night. Besides, the ocean tide turns against them. All have to leave, without Ferdinand's future bride.

When it is entirely dark, save for the stars overhead, and she is sure that all have sailed away, then Miranda comes from her hiding place. She calls through the oak grove for her Caliban, that nature boy who made her girlhood rich, who taught her all the secret pleasures of the island, the fresh springs wherein they bathed together naked, the rabbit warrens, the mushrooms that, when nibbled, turned their world into a golden place.

He came to her, a burly figure wrapped in darkness, but reassuring, and took her to his cave. There they lived, free of all constraint.

Caliban sings a song to his lovely prize.

> The nightingales are singing in
>   The orchards of our mothers,
> While wounds that plagued us long ago
>   Mayhap fester on others.
>
> Summer cozens our repose.
> How we live here no one knows!
> Sea nymphs hourly plight our troth
> Where the gladsome waves do froth.
>   Ding dong! Ding dong bell!

Miranda bore him children. Thus did the words that Shakespeare put into Caliban's mouth come true; for when Prospero accuses Caliban of seeking to violate the honour of his daughter, Caliban laughs and says, 'Thou didst prevent me – I had peopled else the isle with Calibans'. Now the act is accomplished, with mutual consent and entire rapture.

The little ones played among the peaceful dells of the isle, or sported in the sea. Several swam before they could walk. This was the golden age for Miranda and Caliban, there on the island where both had spent their early days, and found each other.

So ten years passed. Until one day, Prince Ferdinand returned. All those years, passed with whorish women, had not dimmed his desire for Miranda. He had become rich upon inheriting the crown of Naples. He dressed well. With hard exercise, he had kept a trim figure. Only his face was now mapped with lines that told his youth was almost spent.

So on his fortieth birthday he came armed with jewels to regain his old love, and fulfil an old dream.

He and she stand facing one another. Miranda holds her latest daughter by the hand and remains defiant, saying nothing.

Ferdinand is quite discomfited. Reality has met his dream. She is no longer the slender maiden whose image has remained frozen in his mind throughout the years.

'Miranda, think you that your brow is still unwrinkled? Your bulky limbs still virginal and slim? Your eye still clear with innocence? Your sweet enchantments now are faded, much as the baseless fabric of a dream is torn by waking. Sleeping with renegades hardly improves your shape. Why should you have my gifts?'

To which Miranda meekly makes response.

'Sir, look at me, and feast your eyes upon fulfilment! I am a wife whose whole experience derides that thing which you affect to prize – my chastity! Eros has a gentler touch than Time, more kisses to the minute. I've been fatted up by love – you boast a deficit of flesh. What eats you, royal Naples prince, so profligate and thin? Desire, ambition, hate? I see the blow-fly in your glance.'

He brings up an arm to hide his face.

In a while, he asks her brokenly why she left him, that day when they were about to sail to Naples, to be wed in a cathedral and live in a palace. The misery of that day still haunts him.

Her answer is mild, but definite. 'I am not ceremony's bride who was informal nature's child.'

She goes on to tell him that at first she had admired him, with his swagger airs and clothes, his flattery. She would be Queen of Naples and she'd wear – oh, she forgets quite what. But when she grew to know him better, she saw how robes and rings and thrones were pageants, mere material things. And in that moment on the shore, about to leave the isle, she saw that she was taking a wrong path through life.

She thought of Caliban . . .

For he it was, despised and beaten, who was her own true friend, without pretence. He it was taught her to laugh, and play a flute. He tamed a hare for her, amused her by turning cartwheels. He named for her the natural treasures of the isle, the fresh springs where they bathed together nude, the rabbit warrens, mushrooms that, when nibbled, quite transformed their world.

'And what's more, foraged in my crack such joyous feelings I had never known before. Before sex had a name we lay together — not once but countless times. So in that moment of decision, I knew I did not need your promises. The island held my happiness, not Naples.'

In misery, Ferdinand flings his presents down. He turns and runs back to the beach. Miranda and Caliban follow, linking hands, to watch him go. He climbs into his boat and starts to row away.

Then he stows the oars and stands up recklessly, to call in a choked voice, 'I loved you once, Miranda . . .'

And Caliban answers, in his pride, 'Then that must be enough.'

His cry returns, now faint beneath the splashing of the waves, to haunt us till our dying day, 'Nothing in life is ever enough . . .'

The gleaming distance bears his boat away.

But that is just what I wrote. And what I lived is quite another thing.

A Matter of Mathematics

It was a funny thing about Joyce Bagreist. She lived on yoghurt and jam sandwiches. She never washed her hair. She was not popular at her university. Yet Bagreist's Short Cut changed the universe. Simply, shockingly, inevitably, irretrievably.

Of course it was a matter of mathematics. Everything has changed.

Back at human beginnings, perception was locked in a shuttered house. One by one, the shutters snapped open, or were forced open. The 'real' world outside was perceived. Because perception – like everything else – evolved.

We can never be sure if all the shutters have yet snapped open.

At one time, 'in the old days', it was well-known that the caves of Altamira in northern Spain had been accidentally discovered by a girl of five. She had wandered from her father. Her father was an archaeologist, and much too busy studying an old stone to notice that his daughter had strayed from his side.

It is easy to imagine the fine afternoon, the old man kneeling by the stone, the young girl picking wild flowers. She finds blue flowers, red ones and yellow. She wanders on, taking little thought. The ground is broken. She attempts to climb a slope. Sand falls away in a toytown version of an avalanche. She sees an opening. She has no fear, but plenty of curiosity. She climbs in. Just a little way. She is in a cave. There she sees on the wall the figure of an animal, a buffalo.

That does frighten her. She climbs out and runs back to her father, crying that she has seen an animal. He abandons his stone and goes to look.

And what he finds is an extensive gallery of scenes, painted by Palaeolithic hunters or magicians, or hunter/magicians. The great artistry of the scenes changes human understanding of the past. We came to believe we comprehended that sympathetic magic when we had in fact failed to do so. Our mind patterns had changed: we were unable to comprehend Palaeolithic thought, however hard we tried. We accepted a scientific, mathematical model into our heads, and had to live by it.

Clues to a true understanding of the universe lie everywhere. One after another, clues are found and, when the time is ripe, can be understood. The great reptiles whose bones lie in the rocks waited there for millions of years to be interpreted. They expanded greatly humanity's knowledge of duration and the planet's duration. Frequently women are associated with such shocks to the understanding, perhaps because they contain magic in their own persons (although there seemed little magic to Joyce Bagreist's person). It was a Mrs Gideon Mantell who discovered the bones of the first reptile to be identified as a dinosaur.

All such discoveries seem little short of miraculous at the time; then they become taken for granted. So it has proved in the case of Bagreist's Short Cut.

It has been forgotten now, but an accident similar to the Altamira accident brought Joyce Bagreist to understand and interpret the signal of the Northern Lights, or *aurora borealis*. For untold years, the lights had been explained away as the interaction of charged particles from the sun with particles in the upper atmosphere. True, the signal was activated by the charged particles: but no one until Bagreist had thought through to the purpose of this phenomenon.

Joyce Bagreist was a cautious little woman, not particularly liked at her university because of her solitary nature. She was slowly devising and building a computer which worked on the colour spectrum rather than on mathematics. Once she had formulated new equations and set up her apparatus, she spent some while preparing for what she visualised might follow. Within the privacy of her house, Bagreist improvised for herself a kind of wheeled space suit, complete with bright headlights, an emergency oxygen supply and a stock of food. Only then did she track along her upper landing, encased inside her novel vehicle, along the measured two point five metres, and through the archway of scanners and transmitters of her apparatus.

At the end of the archway, with hardly a jolt to announce a revolution in thought, she found herself in the crater Aristarchus, on Earth's satellite, the Moon.

It will be remembered that the great Aristarchus of Samos, in whose honour the crater was named, was the first astronomer correctly to read another celestial signal now obvious to us – that the Earth was in orbit about the Sun, rather than vice versa.

There Bagreist was, rather astonished and slightly vexed. According to her calculations, she should have emerged in the crater Copernicus. Clearly her apparatus was more primitive and fallible than she had bargained for.

Being unable to climb out of the crater, she circled it in her home-made suit, feeling pleased with the discovery of what we still call Bagreist's Short Cut – or, more frequently, more simply, the Bagreist.

There was no way in which this brave discoverer could return to Earth. It was left to others to construct an archway on the Moon. Poor Joyce Bagreist perished there in Aristarchus, a last jam sandwich on her lap, perhaps not too dissatisfied with herself. She had radioed to Earth. The signal had been picked up. Space Administration had sent a ship. But it arrived too late for Joyce Bagreist.

Within a year of her death, traffic was pouring through several archways, and the Moon was covered with building materials.

But who or what had left the colour-coded signal in the Arctic skies to await its hour of interpretation?

Of course, the implications of the Bagreist were explored. It became clear that space/time did not possess the same configuration as had been assumed. Another force was operative, popularly known as the Squidge Force. Cosmologists and mathematicians were hard put to explain the Squidge Force, since it resisted formulation in current mathematical systems. The elaborate mathematical systems on which our global civilisation was founded had merely local application: they did not extend even as far as the heliopause. So while the practicalities of Bagreist were being utilised, and people everywhere (having bought a ticket) were taking a short

walk from their home on to the lunar surface, mathematical lacunae were the subject of intense and learned
enquiry.

Two centuries later, I back into the story. I shall try to
explain simply what occurred. But not only does P-L6344
enter the picture; so do Mrs Staunton and General
Tomlin Willetts, and the general's lady friend, Molly
Levaticus.

My name, by the way, is Terry W. Manson, L44/56331.
I lived in Lunar City IV, popularly known as Ivy. I was
General Secretary of Recreationals, working for those who
manufacture IDs, or individual drugs, those enhancing
drugs tailored to personal genetic codes.

I had worked previously for the Luna-based MAW, the
Meteor and Asteroid Watch, which was how I came to
know something of General Willetts' affairs. Willetts was a
big consumer of IDs. He was in charge of the MAW operation, and had been for the previous three years. His last
few months had been taken up with Molly Levaticus, who
had joined his staff as a junior operative and was shortly
afterwards made Private Secretary to the general. In consequence of this closely kept secret affair – known to
many on the base – General Willetts went about in a
dream.

My more serious problem also involved a dream. A golf
ball lying forlorn on a deserted beach may have nothing
outwardly sinister about it. However, when that same
dream recurs every night, one begins to worry. There lay
that golf ball, there was that beach. Both monuments to
perfect stasis, and in consequence alarming.

The dream became more insistent as time went by. It
seemed – I know no other way of expressing it – to move
closer to my vision every night. I became alarmed.

Eventually, I made an appointment to see Mrs Staunton, Mrs Roslyn Staunton, the best-known mentatropist in Ivy.

After asking all the usual questions, involving my general health, my sleeping habits, and so forth, Roslyn – we soon lapsed into first names – asked me what meaning I attached to my dream.

'It's just an ordinary golf ball. Well . . . No, it has markings resembling a golf ball's markings. I don't know what else it could be. And it's lying on its side.'

When I thought about what I was saying, I saw I was talking nonsense. A golf ball has no sides. So it was not a golf ball.

'And it's lying on a beach?' she prompted.

'That's right.'

'So it's not on the Moon.'

'It has nothing to do with the Moon.' But there I was wrong.

'What sort of a beach? A resort beach, for instance?'

'Far from it. An infinite beach. Alienating. Stony. Pretty bleak.'

'You recognise the beach?'

'No. It's an alarming place – well, the way infinity is always pretty alarming. Just an enormous stretch of territory with nothing growing on it. Oh, and the ocean. A sullen ocean. The waves are heavy and leaden – and slow. About one per minute gathers up its strength and slithers up the beach. I ought to time them.'

She said, 'Time is never reliable in dreams.' Then she asked, 'Slithers?'

'Waves don't seem to break properly on this beach. They just subside.' I sat in silence thinking about this desolate yet somehow tempting picture which haunted me. 'I feel in a way I've been there. The sky. It's very heavy and enclosing.'

'So you feel this is all very unpleasant?'

With surprise, I heard myself saying, 'Oh no, I need it, it promises something. Something emerging . . . Out of the sea, I suppose.'

'Why do you wish to cease dreaming this dream if you need it?'

That was a question I found myself unable to answer.

While I was undergoing three sessions a week with Roslyn, the general was undergoing more frequent sessions with Molly Levaticus. And P-L6344 was rushing nearer.

Molly was an intellectual lady, played a silver trumpet, spoke seven languages, was a chess champion, was also highly sexed and inclined to mischief. Dark of hair, with a pert nose. A catch for any man, I'd say. Even General Tomlin Willetts.

The general's wife, Hermione, was blind, and had been since childhood. Willetts was not without a sadistic streak, or how else would he have become a general? We are all blind in some fashion, either in our private lives or in some shared public way; for instance, millions of Earthbound people, otherwise seemingly intelligent, still believe that the Sun orbits the Earth, rather than vice versa. This, despite all the evidence to the contrary and the true facts having been known for centuries.

This type of people would say in their own defence that they believe the evidence of their eyes. Yet we know well that our eyes can see only a small part of the electromagnetic spectrum. All our senses are limited in some fashion. And, because limited, often mistaken. Even 'unshakeable evidence' concerning the nature of the universe was due to take a knock, thanks to P-L6344.

Willetts' sadistic nature led him to persuade his fancy lady, Molly Levaticus, to walk naked about the rooms of his and his wife's apartment, while the blind Hermione was present. I believe she simply enjoyed the sexual mischief of it. Roslyn agreed. It was a prank. But commentators variously saw Molly either as a victim or as a dreadful predatory female.

Nobody considered that the truth, if there was a unitary truth, lay somewhere between the two poles: that there was an affinity between the individuals involved, which is not as unusual as it may appear, between the older man and the younger woman. Molly undoubtedly had her power, as he had his weakness. They played on each other.

And they played cat-and-mouse with Hermione Willetts. She would be sitting at the meal-table, with Willetts placed near by. Into the room would come the naked Levaticus, on tiptoe. Winks were exchanged with Willetts. She would circle the room in a slow dance, hands above her head, showing her unshaven armpits, in a kind of *t'ai chi*, moving close to the blind woman.

Sensing a movement in the air, or a slight noise, Hermione would ask mildly, 'Tomlin, dear, is there another person in the room?'

He would deny it.

Sometimes Hermione would strike out with her stick. Molly always dodged.

'Your behaviour is very strange, Hermione,' Willetts would say, severely. 'Put down that stick. You are not losing your senses, are you?'

Or they would be in the living-room. Hermione would be in her chair, reading a book in Braille. Molly would stick out her little curly pudendum almost in the lady's face. Hermione would sniff and turn the page. Molly would glide to Willetts' side, open his zip, and remove his erect penis, on which her fingers played like a musician with a flute. Then Hermione might lift her blind gaze and ask what her husband was doing.

'Just counting my medals, dearest,' he would reply.

What was poor Hermione's perception of her world? How mistaken was it, or did she prefer not to suspect, being powerless?

But he was equally blind, disregarding the signals from MAW, urging an immediate decision on what to do to deflect or destroy the oncoming P-L6344.

Willetts was preoccupied with his private affairs, as I was preoccupied with my mentatropic meetings with Roslyn. As our bodies went on their courses, so too did the bodies of the solar system.

Apollo asteroids cross the Earth/Moon orbit. Of these nineteen small bodies, possibly the best known is Hermes, which at one time passed the Moon at a distance only double the Moon's distance from Earth. P-L6344 is a small rock, no more than one hundred and ninety metres across. On its previous crossing, the brave astronaut, Flavia da Beltrau do Valle, managed to anchor herself to the rock, planting there a metal replica of the Patagonian flag. At the period of which I am speaking, the asteroid was coming in fast at an inclination of five degrees to the plane of the ecliptic. Best estimations demonstrated that it would impact with the Moon at 23.03 on August 5th, 2208, just a few kilometres north of Ivy. But defensive action was delayed because of General Willetts' other interests.

So why were the computers not instructed by others, and the missiles not armed by subordinates? The answer must lie somewhere in everyone's absurd preoccupation with their own small universes, of which they form the perceived centre. Immersed in Recreationals, they were in any case disinclined to act.

Perhaps we have a hatred of reality. Reality is too cold for us. Perceptions of all things are governed by our own selves. The French master, Gustave Flaubert, when asked where he found the model for the central tragic figure of Emma in his novel, *Madame Bovary*, is said to have replied, 'Madame Bovary? C'est moi.' Certainly Flaubert's horror of life is embodied in his book. The novel stands as an example of a proto-recreational.

Even as the Apollo asteroid was rushing towards us, even as we were in mortal danger, I was looking – under Roslyn's direction – to find the meaning of my strange dream in the works of the German philosopher, Edmund Husserl. Husserl touched something in my soul, for he rejects all assumptions about existence, preferring the subjectivity of the individual's perceptions as a way in which we experience the universe.

A clever man, Husserl. But saying little about what things were really like if our perceptions turned out to be faulty. Or, for instance, if we did not perceive the crisis of an approaching asteroid soon enough.

Running promptly to timetable, P-L6344 struck. By a coincidence, it impacted in the Crater Copernicus, the very crater for which Joyce Bagreist had initially been aiming.

The Moon staggered in its orbit.

Everyone in Ivy fell down. Hermione, groping blindly for her stick, clutched Molly Levaticus's hairy little pudendum and shrieked, 'There's a cat in here!'

Many buildings and careers were ruined, including General Willetts'.

Most lunarians took the nearest Bagreist home. Many feared that the Moon would swan off into outer space under the force of impact. I had my work to do. I disliked the squalid cities of Earth. But primarily I stayed on because Roslyn Staunton stayed, both she and I being determined to get to the bottom of my dream. Somehow, by magical transference, it had become her dream too. Our sessions together became more and more conspiratorial.

At one point I did consider marrying Roslyn, but kept the thought to myself.

After the strike, everyone was unconscious for at least two days. Sometimes for a week. The colour red vanished from the spectrum.

Another strange effect was that my dream of the golf ball lying on its side faded away. I never dreamed it again. I missed it. I ceased visiting Roslyn as a patient. Since she no longer played a professional role in my life, I was able to invite her out to dine at the Earthscape Restaurant, where angelfish were particularly good, and later to drive out with her to inspect the impact site, once things had cooled down sufficiently.

Kilometres of grey ash rolled by as the car drove us westward. Plastic pine trees had been set up on either side of the road, in an attempt at scenery. They ceased a kilometre out of town, where the road forked. Distant palisades caught the slant of sun, transforming them into spires of an alien faith. Roslyn and I sat mute, side by side, pursuing our own thoughts as we progressed. We had switched off the radio. The voices were those of penguins.

'I miss Gauguins,' she said suddenly. 'His vivid expressionist colour. The bloody Moon is so grey – I sometimes wish I had never come here. Bagreist made it all too easy. If it hadn't been for you . . .'

'I have a set of Gauguin paintings on slides. Love his work!'

'You do? Why didn't you say?'

'My secret vice. I have almost a complete set.'

'You have? I thought he was the great forgotten artist.'

'Those marvellous wide women, chocolate in their nudity. The dogs, the idols, the sense of a brooding presence . . .'

She uttered a tuneful scream. 'Do you know *Vairaumati Tei Oa*? The woman smoking, a figure looming behind her?'

'And behind them a carving of two people copulating?'

'God, you do know it, Terry! The sheer colour! The sullen joy! Let's stop and have a screw to celebrate.'

'Afterwards. Fine. His sense of colour, of outline, of pattern. Lakes of red, forests of orange, walls of viridian . . .'

'His senses were strange. Gauguin learned to see everything new. Maybe he was right. Maybe the sand is pink.'

'Funny he never painted the Moon, did he?'

'Not that I know of. It could be pink too.'

We held hands. We locked tongues in each other's mouth. Our bodies forced themselves on each other. Craving, craving. Starved of colour. Cracks appeared in the road. The car slowed.

My thoughts ran to the world Paul Gauguin had discovered and – a different matter – the one he opened up for others. His canvases were proof that there was no common agreement about how reality was. Gauguin was Husserl's proof. I cried my new understanding to Roslyn. 'Reality' was a conspiracy, and Gauguin's images persuaded people to accept a new and different reality.

'Oh God, I am so happy!'

The road began to hump. The tracked vehicle went to dead slow. In a while it said, 'No road ahead', and stopped. Roslyn and I clamped down our helmets, got out and walked.

No one else was about. The site had been cordoned off, but we climbed the wire. We entered Copernicus by the gap which had been built through its walls some years previously. The flat ground inside the crater was shattered. Heat of impact had turned it into glass. We picked our way across a treacherous skating rink. In the centre of the upheaval was a new crater, the P-L6344 crater, from which a curl of smoke rose, to spread itself over the dusty floor.

Roslyn and I stood on the lip of this new crater, looking down. A crust of grey ash broke in one place, revealing a red glow beneath.

'Too bad the Moon got in the way . . .'

'It's the end of something . . .'

There was not much you could say.

She tripped as we made to turn back. I caught her arm and steadied her. Grunting with displeasure, Roslyn kicked at what she had tripped on. A stone gleamed dully.

She brought over her handling arm. Its long metal fingers felt in the churned muck and gripped the object – not a stone. It was rhomboidal – manufactured. In size, no bigger than a vacuum flask. Exclaiming, we took it back to the car.

The P-L6344 rhomboid! Dating techniques showed it to be something over two and a half million years old. It opened when chilled down to 185.333K.

From inside it emerged a complex thing which was at first taken for a machine of an elaborate, if miniature, kind. The machine moved slowly, retracting and projecting series of rods and corkscrew-like objects. Analysis showed it to be made of various semi-metal materials, such as were unknown to us, created from what we would have called artificial atoms, where semiconductor dots contained thousands of electrons. It emitted a series of light flashes.

This strange thing was preserved at 185.333K and studied.

Recreationals got in on the act because research was funded by treating this weird object from the remote past as a form of exhibition. I was often in the laboratory area. Overhearing what people said, as they shuffled in front of the one-way glass, I found that most of them thought it was pretty boring.

At night, Roslyn and I screamed at each other about 'the tourists'. We longed for a universe of our own. Not here, not on the Moon. Her breasts were the most intelligent I ever sucked.

Talking to Roslyn about this strange signalling thing we owned, I must admit it was she who made the perception. 'You keep calling it a machine,' she said. 'Maybe it is a kind of a machine. But it could be living. Maybe this is a survivor from a time when the universe did not support carbon-based life. Maybe it's a pre-biotic living thing!'

'A what?'

'A pre-life living thing. It isn't really alive because it has never died, despite being two million years in that can. Terry, you know the impossible happens. Our lives are impossible. This thing delivered to us is both possible and impossible.'

My instinct was to rush about telling everyone. In particular, telling the scientists on the project. Roslyn cautioned me against doing so.

'There must be something in this for us. We may be only a day or two ahead of them before they too realise they are dealing with a kind of life. We have to use that time.'

My turn to have a brainwave. 'I've recorded all its flashes. Let's decode them, see what they are saying. If this little object has intelligence, then there's a meaning awaiting discovery . . .'

The universe went about its inscrutable course. People lived their inscrutable lives. But Roslyn and I hardly slept, slept only after her sharp little hips had ground into mine. We transformed the flickering messages into sound, we played them backwards, we speeded them up and slowed them down. We even ascribed values to them. Nothing played.

The stress made us quarrelsome. Yet there were moments of calm. I asked Roslyn why she had come to the Moon. We had already read each other, yet did not know the alphabet.

'Because it was easy just to walk through the neighbouring Bagreist, in a way my grandparents could never have imagined. And I wanted work. And—'

She stopped. I waited for the sentence to emerge. 'Because of something buried deep within me.'

She turned a look on me that choked any response I might make. She knew I understood her. Despite my job, despite my career, which hung on me like a loose suit of clothes, I lived for distant horizons.

'Speak, man!' she ordered. 'Read me.'

'It's the far perspective. That's where I live. I can say what you say, "because of something buried deep within me". I understand you with all my heart. Your impediment is mine.'

She threw herself on me, kissing my lips, my mouth, saying, 'God, I love you, I drink you. You alone understand—'

And I was saying the same things, stammering about the world we shared in common, that with love and mathematics we could achieve it. We became the animal with two backs and one mind.

I was showering after a night awake when the thought struck me. This pre-biotic semi-life we had uncovered, buried below the surface of the Moon for countless ages, did not require oxygen, any more than did Roslyn's and my perceptions. What fuel, then, might it use to power its mentality? The answer could only be: *Cold!*

We sank the temperature of the flickering messages, using the laboratory machine when the place was vacated during the hours of night. At 185.332K, the messages went into phase. A degree lower, and they became solid, emitting a dull glow. We photographed them from several angles before switching off the superfrigeration.

What we uncovered was an entirely new mathematical mode. It was a mathematics of a different existence. It underpinned a phase of the universe which contradicted ours, which made our world remote from us, and from our concept of it. Not that it rendered ours obsolete: far from it, but rather that it demonstrated by irrefutable logic that we had not understood how small a part of totality we shared.

This was old grey information, denser by far than lead, more durable than granite. Incontrovertible.

Trembling, Roslyn and I took it – again at dead of night, when the worst crimes are committed – and fed its equations into the Crayputer which governed and stabilised Luna. It was entered and in a flash—

We climbed groaning out of the hole. Here was a much larger Bagreist. As we entered into the flabby light, we saw the far perspective we had always held embedded in us: that forlorn ocean, those leaden waves, and that desolate shore, so long dreamed about, its individual grains now scrunching under our feet.

Behind us lay the ball which had been the Moon, stranded from its old environment, deep in its venerable age, motionless upon its side.

We clasped each other's hands with a wild surmise, and pulled ourselves forth.

THE PAUSE BUTTON

Despite advances in genetic engineering, it seems that human society will never improve. Fortunately, something has been done to remove a few of its stresses. The Pause Button has been invented.

Although our physical world is now fully explored, and automated instruments have charted the planet Mars, a much more complex world has been opened up by science, and its confusion of passageways traversed.

The topography of the brain has at last become understood.

A small firm in Birmingham decided to put the knowledge to practical use. Conrad Barlow owned a motorcycle shop. It happened that he drank once a week with his cousin, Gregory Magee. Both men had a keen interest in football, and supported their local team. Otherwise, their lives were very different. Conrad was an expert on any kind of engine, while Gregory was a surgeon at the local hospital, specialising in cranial and brain injury.

Gregory – known privately to the nurses as 'Mad' Magee because of a slight eccentricity – had to operate on a team member of Birmingham North End, injured in a match. The player, Reggie Peyton, had developed a blood clot in the right temporal lobe. It was easily removed. However, Peyton did not return to consciousness when the anaesthetic wore off. He seemed perfectly fit in all physical aspects. For almost two days he remained in a comatose state. When he woke, he was perfectly well, and returned home. But he did not play again.

Somewhere here was a mystery which Gregory alone perceived. He discussed the matter with Conrad over a pint that Saturday night.

'Excitory transmitters failed to function,' he said.

Conrad drummed his fingers on the bar. 'This was in the right-hand temporal lobe? Greg, isn't that where Cotard's delusion takes place? You remember, we were talking about Cotard the other week?'

From that casual remark onwards, they knew they were on the trail of *something*.

Cotard, the great French psychiatrist, identified a syndrome whereby patients believe themselves to be dead. The illusion persists, despite such evidence to the contrary as heartbeat, lungs functioning perfectly, body temperature sustained. The self-evident impossibility of the notion causes it to break down after a while.

Here was the clue that led to the invention of the Pause Button. Despite its popular nickname, the micro-function that Conrad and Gregory devised was a molecular machine.

A small molecule was sited on a large molecule where, like an enzyme, it bonds. Other molecules are added, until a complex structure is formed. Thus a nanomachine is created which is controlled by molecular tapes responsive to adrenaline rises in the brain of as little as 0.0001 per cent.

When correctly positioned in the right temporal lobe of the brain, the Pause Button, more properly known as the Delay Functional Reflex, has the following function. In a crisis situation, the person with a DFR is given pause. Although the delay is momentary, it allows the person to think about what he intends to do. Our brains have been so constructed that emotion overrides intellect in crisis situations. Anger blots out thought. The DFR circumvents this phylogeneric trait.

Much violence is prevented. Beating the dog, the child, men beating the woman – such things are forestalled. The percentages of male violence against their female partners were alarming: in the U.K., twenty-five per cent, in the U.S.A., twenty-eight per cent. Many such elemental attacks were launched when the woman became pregnant. Since the widespread introduction of DFRs, these figures have dropped to eleven per cent and twelve per cent respectively (there has been a greater take-up in the U.S.A. than the U.K.).

At first, Conrad and Gregory were able to sell their device only to such institutions as prisons, where the insertion of a DFR earned a prisoner a five per cent reduction of sentence.

An enlightened government saw wider opportunities. Motorists were tempted by a reduction in cost of their vehicle licence if they underwent the operation. Road rage became a thing of the past. Accidents rapidly decreased.

The general public became interested. It was pleasant to remain calm. The DFR also prevented hasty words spoken in anger. There was greater harmony between partners than previously. Euphoria became popular.

No longer are we asking, 'Why did I do that?' or, 'What was I thinking about?' We now take the opportunity to know.

Perhaps the most dramatic change came in political habits. Politicians in democracies were elected, in many cases, to solve problems almost beyond the province of politics, such as how to stop wastage of valuable resources, how to assist and educate the disempowered, how to prevent racial tensions. Voters may say they support these ambitions. However, the promise of tax cuts may persuade them to think differently. If a slight reduction in taxes is offered against increased funding of education, it is not infrequently education which goes to the wall.

So politicians utter hypocritical promises. They swear to effect changes that could not be carried though within the five year electoral term. Both sides of the bargain are lulled by false promises.

But now comes the Pause Button effect!

Everyone is given time to consider. So we are becoming more honest, more realistic. We now have time to consider the value of honesty, to weigh the truth behind promises – we who were so accustomed to a diet of lies.

In the year that Conrad Barlow and Gregory Magee received the Nobel Peace Prize, we voted in the United Reality Party to govern the country.

The great challenge now is to link the DFR into the genetic chain, so that its effects become inheritable.

Of course this will change us. Our ramshackle societies will change. Later, fully evolved human beings will look back on today much as we look back on the denizens of the Stone Age.

Three Types
of Solitude

Happiness in Reverse

Judge Beauregard Peach was writing to his estranged wife, Gertrude. Gertrude had her own prosperous career as a lawyer. However, following a number of serious quarrels with her husband, she had taken herself off with their adult daughter, Catherine, to the South of France.

There she was visited by an Oxford man she had known in the past, a well-placed journalist. They sailed and visited restaurants and drank copiously, and she received unwelcome letters from Beauregard.

Beauregard did not plead for her to return. His mind worked in a more sophisticated way. Gertrude knew that way, admired it, feared it.

My dearest Gertrude, (he wrote)

I regret you are not here with me in Oxford, since the case I am now hearing would interest you. It may indeed prove momentous.

We are sitting at Oxford Crown Court. So unusual is the problem that the court is always full to overflowing. The ushers are having difficulties with the crowds which gather outside early in the morning. Reporters are present, not only from the *Oxford Mail*, as one might expect, but from several of the London papers, together with a stringer from the *New York Herald Tribune*.

Traffic comes regularly to a standstill from Magdalen Bridge to the railway station, though 'nothing unusual about that', as a would-be wit has commentèd. Unfortunately, the judge's wife has taken herself away for a holiday, while her husband sits upon the question, What to do with a man, no petty criminal, indeed one of a long line of Oxford eccentrics who intend no harm, who has invented a new, if rather wooden, race or species, the reproduction rate of which threatens humanity? (Incidentally, what a conundrum to face an ageing man rendered suddenly impotent by his wife's unfaithfulness! I am sure you must laugh to think of it.)

The case has been unprecedented; I consider myself fortunate to sit on it. We must think it one of the perks of living in Oxford – rather as if we had been present last century at that evolution debate presided over by Bishop Wilberforce.

The world is crowded enough as it is; sufficient ecological damage has already been done to our natural habitat. Here before me is someone responsible for more, much more, of the same.

The accused, Donald Maudsley, is an ordinary enough fellow as regards appearances. A little beard, rather beaky nose, fair hair tied back in a short pony tail. Of average height, or under. A melancholy man, but not unintelligent. An old Oriel man, in fact.

He has a way of telling his story in the third person, which I found rather irritating at first. It becomes evident that he suffers from dissociation of personality.

A transcript of his deposition runs as follows:

After gaining his degree, this little man, by name Donald Maudsley, went into Earth Sciences. He attended the Brazil Conference, after which he disappeared into the wilds of South America. This is the essence of his story.

This little man came to live on the edge of an undiscovered rain forest which swept right down to the South Pacific ocean. The sun shone, the winds blew, the rains came and went. Days and years passed. No one knew where this man was. He had no contact with the outside world. No boat ever visited the shore. No plane ever passed overhead. It proved a congenial place in which to undergo a crisis of identity.

The little man collected discarded sunsets. He swept them up every evening when they were spent, and kept them in a big golden cage in the depths of the forest.

Although he often sang to himself, generally a folk song about a hermit polar bear, he remained lonely. He rarely met with another living thing, apart from crabs on the beach. Occasionally a white bird, an albatross, flew by overhead. The sight merely increased his feeling of solitude. The

solitude pierced his being and became a part of
him.

Early one morning, he cut down a forest tree.
From a section of the tree he fashioned a
ventriloquist's dummy. He called the dummy Ben.
He imbued Ben with an illusion of life for the sake
of company.

The man and the doll held long conversations
together, sitting on the trunk of the felled tree. In
the main, they discussed morality, and whether
there was a necessity for it. The little man had a
stern morality which had served to shape his life.
While up at Oriel, he had met a handsome and
intelligent young woman, the daughter of foreign
royalty. He had been in love with her. But when she
had done her best to persuade him to make love to
her, he had refused and shunned her company.

Her response to rejection had been one of fury
and vituperation.

He had then studied at Black Friars to take holy
orders, but once more felt unable to carry his
wishes through. In his despair, he felt it was
morality which had driven him apart from all
human company.

The dummy sometimes became passionate on the
subject, believing morality to be merely a failure in
relationships. For a wooden thing, the dummy was
surprisingly eloquent. It ran about the beach, such
was its strength of conviction. But these arguments
led nowhere, like the beach.

Gertrude, I am dining in hall this evening, and
must change my clothes. My scout is here. I will
write to you again soon, to give you an account of

the conversations which took place, according to
Maudsley, between him and his dummy.
    With love,

Gertrude felt herself moved to write Beauregard a note in
return.

> The case on which you are sitting holds curious
> echoes of our own past. This fellow Maudsley must
> ache to find love in a loveless and godless universe.
> Yet, according to his account, he can find it only
> with a thing of wood. You will recall how
> Hippolytus spurns the amatory approach of
> Phaedra, his step-mother, with priggish coldness.
> Both die.
>   This must provoke your own memory, causing
> you to look back upon the seeds of our present
> difficulties. I wish to hear no more about the case.
>   Gertrude

Nevertheless, the judge wrote again to his absent wife.

> The case continues. We are now into the fourth day.
>   Maudsley claims that his treatment of the
> dummy, Ben, as an independent entity was the
> cause of its increasing semblance of life. He built
> the dummy a small hut next to his own, on a cliff
> above the beach. When he cooked a crab, or a fish,
> he always served a portion to the dummy, who took
> it away to 'eat' in private.
>   Gradually, he claims, they fell into discussing
> more personal topics. The dummy had no past life
> to talk about, although it came out strongly for a

belief in abstaining from meat and growing upwards, sprouting foliage and fruit as you went. This was like a religion with it.

When the man tried to contradict it on this score, the dummy claimed that bearing fruit was the moral way to live, since it was asexual. A pineapple was a symbol of morality, true morality.

One day, the following conversation took place. Maudsley said, 'You cannot argue that asexual reproduction is superior to sexual reproduction. We are different kinds of people, and have to employ whatever methods God has placed at our disposal to increase our kind. To argue otherwise is childish.'

'I'm a child at heart,' said the dummy, striking its chest.

'But you don't possess a heart.'

The dummy regarded him strangely. 'What do you know of my life? Unlike you, I spring from the earth itself. I repress my feelings because I was born of a tree. Trees, in my limited experience, are very dispassionate. I've been so private, I behave so woodenly. I desire to have a heart. But then –' this was said after some thought – 'don't you find that hearts make you sad?'

Maudsley stared meditatively out to sea, to the ocean which possessed something of the blankness of eternity. 'Mm. Something certainly makes me sad. Something hard to define. I always considered it was just the passage of time, not my heart.'

The dummy gave a scornful snigger. 'Time doesn't pass. That's just a human myth. Time's all round us, like some kind of jelly. It's just human life that passes.'

'But what I'm trying to say is that I don't really know what makes me sad.'

'You can't have much knowledge of yourself, then!' said the doll. 'Nothing makes *me* sad, except perhaps a splinter in my buttocks.'

It took a pace or two along the shore, its hands clasped behind its back. Without looking at the man, it said, 'Nope, I'm never sad. Never have been, not even when I was a sapling. I can imagine sadness, like a kind of sawdust. It worries me when you claim you're sad. You're like a god to me, you know that? I can't bear your sadness.'

The Oriel man gave a sad little laugh. 'That's why I try not to tell you about all the grief and longing in my heart.'

The dummy came and sat by the man, resting its chin in its hand. 'I didn't mean to upset you. It's really none of my business.'

'Maybe it is your business.'

A silence fell between them. Over the wide expanse of ocean, another sunset was gathering up its strength to happen, searching in its palette for a brighter gold.

The dummy broke the silence. 'So what's this "sad" business mean, anyway? I mean, how often do you feel like doing it?'

'Sad? Oh, sadness is just happiness in reverse. We humans have to put up with it. Just being human is an awful burden to bear.'

'You keep on doing it? Is that why you feel compelled to collect all these old secondhand sunsets?'

But Maudsley became annoyed at being quizzed

by a mere doll. 'Go away, please! Leave me in peace. You're pathetic, and your questions are meaningless!'

'How can they be meaningless? My questions are your questions, after all.'

'By what logic do you reach that conclusion?'

The dummy replied, 'I'm only your echo, when all's said and done.'

The man had never considered the matter in that way. It occurred to him that perhaps all his life he had only been hearing echoes of himself, and that his morality, on which he had once prided himself, was merely a refusal to permit other people into his life.

He left the doll on the beach, and went to see how the sunset was getting on. As he dragged its discarded colours to the cage in the middle of the rainforest, he saw that the other sunsets he had salved were slowly darkening with time, like old newspapers or discarded flags.

When Gertrude received this account from her estranged husband, she became furious. She was convinced that he was making up the Maudsley case. She phoned and left a message on the answerphone in Beauregard's college rooms, ordering him not to communicate with her on the subject again.

However, the judge sent his wife another letter, excusing himself by saying he imagined that she might care to hear about the conclusion of the case.

Next morning, as Maudsley walked alone along the sand, a motorboat came roaring towards the shore

and a woman jumped out on to the beach. She wore
a white chino suit and had a leather belt with a
holstered gun about her waist. Although she
behaved in an athletic way, he saw when she came
close that she was quite old. Her neck had withered.
There were liver spots dotting her arms and hands.
But the smile on her lined cheeks was good and her
hair was dyed blond.

'Found you at last,' she said. 'I'm from the Chile
Forestry Commission. I've come to rescue you.'

He was bemused, asking her shyly if she was the
woman he had loved and rejected long ago in his
Oriel days.

She laughed. 'Life isn't as tidy as all that.
Besides, I was at Wadham. Hop into the boat.'

Maudsley thought about his dummy and about
the store of spent sunsets. Then he hopped into the
boat.

There his deposition ended.

Ladies and gentlemen of the jury (I said), through
this man's negligence, the dummy people now
number many thousands. The original dummy
reproduced itself asexually, as his descendants
continue to do. They have now ruined the
rainforest – cut most of it down for their bodies –
and that part of the world is completely darkened
by guttering sunsets.

A sentence of life imprisonment for crimes
against ecology would seem to be appropriate.

That's the end of my letter to you today, my dear
Gertie. Of course I feel lonely without you,
otherwise I would not waste my time inventing
fables. I hope you and Catherine are having a happy

spell by the sea, and will soon make up your minds to return to Oxford. Encaenia takes place in ten days; it would be so convenient if you were to accompany me – it's to be held in All Souls this year.

You are the hope and inspiration of my life; I cherish your beauty and the loveliness of your soul. Come back soon!

With love,
Your Beau

II
A SINGLE-MINDED ARTIST

Arthur Scunnersman bought a mansion in the hills behind Antibes. He rented a house in Santa Barbara. He bought a yacht in Nice which never left harbour. He threw lavish parties in London, Paris and New York. He gave the University of Oxford two million dollars for a new art institute to be built on the site of the Radcliffe Infirmary. His clothes were newly bought every day.

Arthur Scunnersman was everywhere. His face appeared everywhere. His women friends were many. He treated each one well, but casually; he was uninterested in their inner lives. It was rumoured that on occasions he slept between a lady and her son.

The breath of scandal made him even more interesting.

Arthur Scunnersman was the artist of his age. He had become famous while still up at Oxford. His paintings and sketches commanded vast sums. His scenic designs for movies and ballets were immensely well paid. And his subjects were so various. There seemed nothing he could not do. The name Scunnersman was on everyone's lips.

His friends noted that he would disappear for weeks at a time. He would reappear with new works, abstracts, representationals, portraits . . . On his return to society, he would throw a party. Everyone attended who had the privilege to be invited. Arthur himself sang at such parties. Sometimes he sang songs he had composed on the spur of the moment. Everyone was charmed, touched, amused. Records were issued of his music, with Arthur singing the songs. Everyone bought them. What a magician he was!

Certainly he was diverse. It was the astonishing diversity of his artwork that most charmed the world — that glowing, fashionable, wealthy world which was so captivated by Arthur Scunnersman and all he seemed to stand for, effortless success above all.

Until one month an influential art critic criticized his diversity as rootlessness. Then Arthur was gone. The world's reporters swore to track him down. They never found him.

They did not think to look in a small Norwegian town twenty kilometres south of Oslo. The town was called Dykstad. The house Scunnersman bought was ordinary, and stood in an ordinary street, opposite the post office.

In the Dykstad house, Scunnersman lived in solitude with a housekeeper, a woman by name Bea Bjørklund. Bea was a country woman. Strange to relate, she had never heard the name of Scunnersman. But she knew a great deal about mackerel fishing.

Bea was plain and placid and given to plumpness, and her blond hair was kept plaited and rolled about her head, so that it resembled an ornamental bread loaf. Her teeth were good, her eyes blue. She washed and cooked and cleaned for Scunnersman, and, after two months had passed, she succumbed to his entreaties, let down her long hair and entered his bed.

She insisted that they made love in the missionary position. She reached orgasm quickly and calmly. They lived lives of strictly regulated mediocrity. Oxford was never mentioned. Scunnersman did nothing. Occasionally, Scunnersman would go for a walk in the neighbourhood – just as far as the old stone bridge and back. He did not take drugs or drink, as formerly, although Bea sometimes persuaded him to enjoy a glass of akavit with her in the evening, before they went to bed.

Sometimes they drove to the coast in her old rusty Ford and went mackerel fishing on the deep and restless North Sea. Bea taught Scunnersman how to hold a rod. Soon, he was also able to catch mackerel, though never as many as she.

He did not paint. He had no paints in Dykstad.

When Christmas came, he went to the big local store up the street and bought Bea some lacy French underwear. Bea went to the big local store up the street and bought Scunnersman a wooden case of oil paints and brushes.

He opened it with astonishment.

'What gave you this idea?'

She showed two pretty dimples as she replied, 'I thought perhaps you might like to take up painting as a hobby. I once saw an artist on television and he looked quite a lot like you. They said he was very successful.'

'Did they now?'

'Maybe you could be successful like him, if you tried. You got good at catching mackerel, that's sure!' She laughed, showing her pretty gums and teeth.

He kissed her and suggested she try on the underwear. He would watch.

On the twelfth day of Christmas, he decided he would paint. One corner of the sparse living room particularly attracted him. It contained a shelf with some books propped up against a heavy stone vase, an old armchair, purple with a red cushion on it, and a little window which looked out on the small patch of land where they grew vegetables, mainly cabbages.

He began slowly to paint. The brush on the canvas was strange to his touch. Bea watched the process without comment.

He asked her over his shoulder what he had asked her before, 'What gave you the idea?'

This time she said with a smile, 'People in the village find it bad that we live together without marriage. So I make you out to be an artist. Then they do not worry. They expect nothing else from artists.'

He rose and kissed her ripe lips.

She was sceptical about the painting when it was finished. 'It's nice. But it's not quite like the real thing.'

'But what would be the point of it being exactly like the real thing?'

The next day, he painted the same corner of the room as previously. Bea's response was as before.

He was amused. He painted the corner of the room over and over. She was never entirely satisfied.

When he had produced his hundredth canvas, she kissed him tenderly, suggesting he gave up. 'You'll never be a success . . .'

But Arthur Scunnersman was just beginning to enjoy himself.

III
TALKING CUBES

War had followed war. Civil war had come with destructive ferocity. My adopted country was in ruins. Many hundreds of thousands of people had died. Many fine buildings had been destroyed. Many hovels had gone. Whole towns were now mere rubble. People were homeless. Many lived under sheets of plastic and boiled water on fires built of twigs. Many died in their sleep, of anger or sorrow or injury.

I had returned there attached to a peace-keeping force, as an Oxfam official. No longer young, I found this country I had loved, where I once enjoyed an intense love affair, had succumbed to old age. How was it to grow young again? How were the minds of the people to be rejuvenated? How were north and south ever to live in harmony again?

Enemy landmines were still hidden in the open country, waiting to blow off the legs of peasants and passers-by. Enemy machines still prowled amid the desolate streets of towns. These technological crabs remained untiring in their programmed malice, and would fire laser beams at anything that moved, whether from north or south. I volunteered to officiate in the task of detecting and dismantling them.

One fine October weekend, I had to attend a multiethnic peace conference in the capital city. A fine new international hotel had been built in an area still remaining moderately intact. Something resembling what we call 'normality' – our Western version of normality – had been established there. Our version included baths and showers and meals for which one sat down at tables to eat. Meals for which one paid with plastic credit cards.

On my first evening in the hotel, I met in the bar a woman who had studied with me at university. Later, we had met again in the foreign capital, before the divisions in the country erupted into civil war. Her name was Sushla Klein. A heavily built man with a shaved head accompanied her.

My heart seemed to leap. I stood stock still. She was seated at a table, looking up at the man, who was standing with his broad shoulders turned to me. Behind them on the wall was a panoramic picture of storks, flying or preening, against a black background. With terrible force, the thought came to me how everything had changed: not only the circumstances of a once prosperous country, not only my circumstances, but no doubt Sushla's circumstances as well. However hard my life had been since we parted, her life had probably been at least as difficult – this precious woman once destined for a quiet scholarly life. Something in the look of her partner's thickset body told me that she had few choices, perhaps few desirable choices, in her current way of living.

So I stood there, uncertain whether or not to retreat. The joy and pain of an old love was upon me.

The thickset man took a chair, still with his back to me. So I could see Sushla less in profile, more in full face, as she turned her gaze on him.

Sushla, I saw, had grown much older – as had I. She was from the south, whereas I was from the north. Nevertheless, we had once enjoyed an intense love affair. I say we enjoyed it; but the enforced secrecy of our love tore us apart; it was an extraordinary mixture of fear, triumph, admiration and sheer lust. We had both been proud to take a lover from the rival race; but there had been peace then, of a kind, and hope for the future, of a kind.

Memories of that past time overwhelmed me as our eyes met. Sushla excused herself from the man she was with and came gladly towards me. He sat glaring at us.

'Sushla, after so many years . . .'

'Oh, was it not all just yesterday?'

We sat in a corner of the salon and drank slow beers together. We were formal with each other, and rather at a loss for words.

'Although it's a coincidence that we meet here,' she said, 'I am better prepared for it than you, as it happens.'

I looked a question at her. There were streaks of grey in her hair.

She produced from a carrier bag a small transparent cube, perhaps ten centimetres to a side. She pushed the ashtray away, setting the cube on the table between us. Looking sometimes directly at me, and sometimes at the perspex cube, she said, 'I have had the afternoon off duty. I wandered through the old streets in the ancient quarter. As I went, I thought of you, and how we had once walked there together. I loved the city at that time. It seemed so full of vigour. Most of the stalls have gone now. Then, of course, it became the capital of an enemy power, the north. And you were gone. Well, times were different when we were at university, weren't they? Better, certainly.'

'Very much better, Sushla.' Her hand lay on the table. I covered it with mine.

'This cube – they were known as holocubes in their day – turned up in a junk shop just along the road and down the first alleyway to the left. I bought it because it so happens that I had found its double in a shop in a south town some while ago. So much for synchronicity . . . Now I have the pair. It's a miracle that both have survived amid so much destruction. Both still work. I shall take them back to Oxford with me next week.'

'You're going back to Oxford?'

'My daughter works at the Ashmolean Museum, in the print department. But you didn't know I had a daughter.' She flashed me a smile from under her eyelashes. 'Not by you, I may add.'

A little dart of jealousy coursed through my being.

'The other cube is in my room, the one I bought earlier. I wish you to see them both working. We can plug them in there. I don't imply anything else by inviting you up to my room. We're too old for all that stuff. Drained of love. At least I am. Nor can I forget you were recently my enemy, or one of them. And the atrocities your people committed against mine.'

'Not my people. I don't *have* people any more.'

'Yes, you do. It's written all over you. England. Oxford.'

'Oh, that! No, I just have mines.' I explained what my occupation was. 'Those mines were laid by both sides. Despite the peace, they continue to kill and maim.'

'Like old grudges.' Sushla smiled sadly. She watched as the man she had been with – possibly her husband – violently stubbed out a cigarette and left the hotel through the glass doors.

I accompanied her up to her room. I was jaded and glad to have someone to talk to – her above all others. A man's tropical suit hung on a cupboard door. His shaving kit lay on a side table. The bed was dishevelled.

Sushla phoned room service for coffee. Decaffeinated.

I stood apart from her. My desire was no longer for her, only for our past, our mutual past, when our beds had been permanently dishevelled.

I did vaguely remember the holocube craze. Lovers

liked them. When the cubes were switched on, a head appeared inside, looked lifelike, spoke, smiled, sometimes wept. The illusion was simply achieved: a hologrammed image of the subject was inscribed on a collapsed germanium-alloy core. It sprang to life when current was passed through it, speaking via loudspeakers concealed in its base. If another person had a similar holocube, the two heads could be made to appear to converse together.

Sushla switched on one of the cubes. The head of a woman with short raven hair, red lips, and a pert nose appeared. She did not move, remaining frozen in the block of artificial ice. The image was rather grainy.

When the other cube was switched on, a male head appeared, young, perky, with broad cheek bones. From an oilskin cap on his head, blond curls protruded. He too was immobile.

I recognised the portraits of ourselves when young. Dread overcame me. That had been she. That had been me.

Sushla moved the cubes closer together and made the two heads, the man and the woman, face each other.

The images began to speak.

The young woman opened falteringly, but almost at once began an outpouring of love.

'. . . I am unable to tell you how much I love you. At home, a brook of fresh water flows by our little house. My love for you is like that – always clear, always renewed. I have never felt before what I feel for you, not for any man. Oh my darling, I know I will always, always, love you and crave your company.'

The man's image was sharper. It was easier to hear what he was saying.

'These are hard times. The situation grows worse. Our politicians must be blind or mad. This house came under rifle fire last night. I want to tell you I still love you, but it is impossible to visit you now. But I must let you know I am thinking of you.'

He paused. The woman spoke again. 'You were in my arms only last night. All night long you were in my arms. How wonderful it was! You know I give myself to you entirely, without reserve, as the ground drinks the summer rain. Be mine for ever, my darling, and – Happy Birthday!'

The male smiled with some tenderness. He spoke English with a concise Oxford intonation.

'The vows we took two years ago remain valid. It's just that I cannot get a permit any more to travel in the south. I'm sick of the whole situation. In fact, I have to tell you – I'm leaving our country, this country suddenly full of disputation. I'm going abroad before things get any worse . . .'

As he mastered his feelings, the woman spoke again. 'Oh, thank you, my darling, for saying you can come tomorrow. We can stay together in my cousin's room. She is away. I will be open to you. Indeed, just to say these happy things, I feel myself already opening. Oh, my darling lover, come to my arms, to my bed. Tomorrow we'll be together again.'

The man said, 'It's ghastly that things have turned out this way. More than we bargained for, eh? Still, there were always differences between us. Your ways were more – well, backward, than ours in the north. You should have come here when I invited you. Not that I blame you. We should have foreseen that civil war was brewing. So – farewell, dear Sushla!'

Sushla's image said, 'Yes, I'll be here waiting for you. Not a cloud shall mar our love for one another. That I swear! . . . I am unable to tell you how much I love you. At home, a brook of fresh water flows by our little house. My love for you is like that – always clear, always renewed. I have never—'

Sushla switched off the cubes. 'After that they just go on repeating themselves. Saying their little piece over and over again – those protestations of love.'

With tears burning in my eyes, I said, uneasily, 'Of course, his holocube was recorded some months after hers. When things had become so much worse . . .'

She buried her face in her hands. 'Oh, we know they are not really conversing, those two, those ghosts of our young selves. Their pre-programmed speeches are triggered by pauses in the other's monologues. But oh, it cuts so deep—' Dry sobs choked off her words.

In guilt and sorrow, I said, 'Sushla, I remember cutting that cube. Having to part hurt me just as much as it did you . . .'

When I put an arm about her shoulder, she gently detached it.

'I know that,' she said, looking up angrily, her face stained with tears. 'What happened to us was just in the nature of things.'

I clutched one of her hands. 'The nature of things.'

She gave a kind of laugh. 'How I hate the nature of things!'

When I tried to kiss her lips, she turned her head away. I pleaded, then our lips met, as once they had done. Though they remained together, lip against lip, breath against breath, this time it was not as prelude but rather as finale.

As I made my way downstairs – the lifts were not working – I thought, the war is over now. Like my youth.

I had not stayed for the coffee to arrive. Sushla remained in her room with the old cubes, old words, old emotions.

STEPPENPFERD

From a cosmological perspective, the sun was a solitary, isolated on the fringes of its galaxy. It was a supergiant. The supergiant belonged in spectral class K5. Seen more closely, it appeared as a dull, smoky globe, a candle about to gutter out, the smoke consisting of myriads of particles dancing in the solar magnetic storm.

Despite its size, it was a cold thing, registering no more than 3,600K. Nevertheless, as a supergiant, it had nurtured sick supergiant fancies in the creatures dependent on it. All about its girth, stretching far out along the plane of the ecliptic, a series of artificial spheres moved in attendance. Each of these spheres contained captive solar systems.

The species which brought the spheres over vast distances, to the supergiant, called themselves the Pentivanashenii, a word that eons ago had meant 'those who once grazed'. This species had cannibalised their own planets and gone forth into the great matrix of space, returning to their home star only to deliver their prizes into captive orbit.

Father Erik Predjin walked out of the dormitory into the early light. In a short while, the monastery bell would toll and his twelve monks and as many novices would rise and go into the chapel for First Devotions. Until then, the little world of the island was his. Or rather, God's.

The low, damp cold came through the birches at him. Father Predjin shivered inside his habit. He relished the bite of dawn. With slow steps, he skirted the stack of adzed timbers designated for the re-roofing of the chapel, the piled and numbered stones which would eventually form part of the rebuilt apse. Ever and again, he looked up at the fabric of the old building to which, with God's guidance and his own will, he was restoring spiritual life.

The monastery was still in poor condition. Some of its foundations dated from the reign of Olav the Peaceful in the eleventh century. The main fabric was of later date, built when the Slav Wends had sought refuge on the island.

What Father Predjin most admired was the southern façade. The arched doorway was flanked by blind arcading with deeply stepped moulded columns. These were weather-worn but intact.

'Here,' Father Predjin often told the so-called tourists, 'you may imagine the early monks trying to recreate the face of God in stone. He is grand, ready to allow entrance to all who come to him, but sometimes blind to our miseries. And by now perhaps the Almighty is worn down by the uncertain earthly weather.'

The tourists shuffled at this remark. Some looked

upwards, upwards, where, hazily beyond the blue sky, a sweep of metal sphere could be seen.

The father felt some small extra contentment this morning. He made no attempt to account for it. Happiness was a sort of bi-product, simply something that occurred in a well-regulated life. Of course, it was autumn, and he always liked autumn. Something about this time, when the leaves began to flee before a northern breeze and the days shortened, gave an extra edge to existence. One was more aware of the great spirit which informed the natural world.

A cock crowed, celebrating the morning's freshness.

He turned his broad back on the ochre-painted building and walked down towards the shore by the paved path he had helped the brothers build. Here, he made his way along by the edge of the water. This meeting of the two elements of land and water was celebrated by a cascade of stones and pebbles. They had been shed from the flanks of retreating glaciers. Those mighty grindstones had polished them so that they lay glistening in the morning light, displaying, for those who cared to look, a variety of colours and origins. No less than the monastery, they were proof for the faithful of a Guiding Hand. A Guiding Hand that had nevertheless allowed itself to be transported across a hundred thousand light years . . .

A dead fish lay silvery among the cobbles, the gentle lap of the waves of the lake giving it a slight lifelike movement. Even in death, it had beauty.

Walking steadily, the father approached a small jetty. An old wooden pier extended a few metres into Lake Mannsjo, dripping water into its dark reflection. To this pier workers would come and, later, another boat with extra-galactic tourists. Directly across the water, no more than a kilometre away, was the mainland and the small town of Mannjer, from which the boats would arrive. A grey slice of pollution spread in a wedge from above the town, cutting across the black inverted image of mountains.

The father studied the mountains and the roofs of the town. How cunningly they resembled the real thing which once had been. He crossed himself. At least this little island had been preserved, for what reason he could not determine. Perhaps the day would come when all returned to normal – if he persevered in prayer.

On the water margin of the island lay old oil drums and remains of military equipment. The island had, until five years ago, been commandeered by the human military for their own purposes. Father Predjin had erased most of the reminders of that occupation: the graffiti in the chapel, the bullet holes in the walls, the shattered trees. He was slow to permit these last military remains to be cleared. Something told him the old rusty landing-craft should remain where it was, half sunk in the waters of the lake. Now that it had ceased to function, it was not out of harmony with its surroundings. Besides, no harm was done in reminding both the brothers and the alien visitors of past follies – and the present uncertain nature of the world. Of the world and, he added to himself, of the whole solar system, now encased in that enormous sphere and transported . . . He knew not where.

Somewhere far beyond the galaxy. But not beyond the reach of God?

He breathed deeply, pleased by the lap-lap-lap of the waters of the lake. He could look west from his little island – the Lord's and his – to what had been Norway and a distant railway line. He could look east to the mountains of what had been Sweden. Lake Mannsjo lay across the border between the two countries. Indeed, the imaginary line of this border, as projected by rulers plied in Oslo and Stockholm ministerial offices, cut across the Isle of Mannsjo and, indeed, right through the old monastery itself. Hence its long occupation by the human military, when territorial opinions had differed and the two Scandinavian countries had been at loggerheads.

Why had they quarrelled? Why had they not imagined . . . well . . . the unimaginable?

He knew the skimpy silver birches growing among the stones on the shore, knew one from the next: was amused to think of some as Norwegian, some as Swedish. He touched them as he went by. The mist-moistened papery bark was pleasing to his hand.

Now that the military had left, the only invaders of Mannsjo were those tourists. Father Predjin had to pretend to encourage their visits. A small boat brought them over, a boat which left Mannjer on the mainland promptly every summer morning, seven days a week, and permitted the beings two hours ashore. In that time, the tourists were free to wander or pretend to worship. And the novices, selling them food and drink and crucifixes, made a little money to help with the restoration fund.

The father watched the boat coming across the water and the grotesque horse-like beings in it slowly taking on human shape and affecting human clothing.

August was fading from the calendar. Soon there would be no more tourists. Mannsjo was less than five degrees south of the Arctic Circle. No tourists came in the long dark winter. They copied everything that had once been, including behaviour.

'I shall not miss them,' said the father, under his breath,

looking towards the distant shore. 'We shall work through the winter as if nothing has happened.' He recognised that he would miss women visitors however. Although he had taken the vow of chastity many years previously, God still permitted him to rejoice at the sight of young women, their flowing hair, their figures, their long legs, the sound of their voices. Not one of the order – not even pretty young novice Sankal – could match the qualities of women. Antelope qualities. But, of course, an illusion; in reality there were seven black ungainly limbs behind every deceiving pair of neat legs.

The beings entered his mind. He knew it. Sometimes he sensed them there, like mice behind the panelling of his room.

He turned his face towards the east, closing his eyes to drink in the light. His countenance was lean and tanned. It was the face of a serious man who liked to laugh. His eyes were generally a grey-blue, and the scrutiny he turned on his fellow men was enquiring but friendly: perhaps more enquiring than open, like shelves of books in a library, whose spines promise much but reveal little of their contents. It had been said by those with whom Father Predjin had negotiated for the purchase of the island that he confided in no one, probably not even his God.

His black hair, as yet no more than flecked by grey, was cut in pudding-basin fashion. He was clean-shaven. About his lips played a sort of genial determination; his general demeanour also suggested determination. In his unself-conscious way, Erik Predjin did not realise how greatly his good looks had eased his way through life, rendering that determination less frequently exercised than would otherwise have been the case.

He thought of a woman's face he had once known, asking himself, Why were men not happier? Had not men and women been set on Earth to make one another happy? Was it because humanity had failed in some dramatic way that this extraordinary swarm of beings had descended, to wipe out almost everything once regarded as permanent?

How was it that the world was so full of sin that it was necessary to destroy it? Now those who sequestered themselves on Mannsjo would continue to do Him reverence. Attempt in their frailty to do Him reverence. To save the world and restore it to what once it was, and make it whole and happy again. Without sin.

Cobbles crunched under his sandals. Hugging his body against the cold, he turned away from the water, up another path which climbed round a giant boulder. Here in a sheltered dell, hens clucked. Here were gardens where the Order grew vegetables – potatoes especially – and herbs and kept bees. All barely enough to sustain the company, but the Almighty approved of frugality. As the father walked among them, casting an expert gaze over the crops, the monastery bell started to toll. Without quickening his pace, he went on, under the apple trees, to his newly repaired church.

He said aloud as he went, clasping his hands together, 'Thank you, O Lord, for another of your wonderful days through which we may live. Protect us from the Penti-vanashenii. And bless my fellow workers, that they also may taste your joy.'

After the morning prayers came breakfast. Homemade bread, fish fresh from the lake, well water. Enough to fill the belly.

Shortly after ten in the morning, Father Predjin and two of the brothers went down to the quay to meet the morning boat bringing the workers from Mannjer. The workers were voluntary labour. They appeared to include not only Scandinavians but men, mainly young, from other parts of Europe, together with a Japanese who had come to visit Mannsjo as a tourist two years ago and had stayed. While he was awaiting novitiate status, he lodged in Mannjer with a crippled woman.

Oh, they all had their stories. But he had seen them from his window, when they thought no one was looking, revert into that lumpish shape with those great trailing hands, seven-fingered, grey in colour.

This was the father's secret: since he knew that these beings were asymmetrical, and not symmetrical, or nearly so; as were human beings, he understood that God had turned his countenance from them. In consequence, they were evil.

The monks welcomed the fake workers and blessed them. They were then directed to the tasks of the day. Few needed much instruction. Plasterers, carpenters and stone masons carried on as previously.

Should I allow such alien and God-hating beings to participate in the construction of God's edifice? Will He curse us all for permitting this error?

Now a little urgency was added to the workers' usual businesslike manner; winter was coming. Over the drum of the main dome an almost flat tiled roof was being installed, closing it against the elements. There was no money at present for the copper-clad dome it was hoped for, provided funds were forthcoming.

When the father had seen that all were employed, he returned to the main building and climbed a twisting stair to his office on the third floor.

It was a narrow room, lit by two round windows and furnished with little more than an old worm-eaten desk and a couple of rickety chairs. A crucifix hung on the whitewashed wall behind the desk.

One of the novices came up to talk to Father Predjin about the question of heating in the winter. The problem arose every year at this time. As usual it remained unresolved.

Immediately next came Sankal. He must have been waiting on the stairs outside the door.

His father gestured to him to take a seat, but the young man preferred to stand.

Sankal stood, twisting his hands about his rough-woven habit, shy as ever, but with the air of a young man who has something important to say and looks only for an opening.

'You wish to leave the order?' Father Predjin said, laughing to show he was joking and merely offering the chance for a response.

Julius Sankal was a pale and pretty youth with down on his upper lip. Like many of the other novices in Mannsjo, he had been given refuge by Predjin because the rest of the globe was disappearing.

In those days, Predjin had stood by his church and looked up at the night sky, to see the stars disappear as the sphere encased them bit by bit. And as surely, the world was disappearing, bit by bit, to be replaced by a cheap replica – perhaps a replica without mass, to facilitate transport. Such things could only be speculated upon, with a burdened sense of one's ignorance and fear.

Sankal had arrived at Mannjer in the snow. And later had stolen a boat in order to cross to the island, to throw himself at the mercy of the ruinous monastery, and of its master. Now he had the job of baking the monastery's bread.

'Perhaps it is necessary I leave,' the youth said. He stood with downcast eyes. Father Predjin waited, hands resting, lightly clasped, on the scarred top of his desk. 'You see . . . I cannot explain. I am come to a wrong belief, father. Very much have I prayed, but I am come to a wrong belief.'

'As you are aware, Julius, you are permitted to hold any one of a number of religious beliefs here. The first important thing is to believe in a god, until you come to see the true God. Thus we light a tiny light in a world utterly lost and full of darkness. If you leave, you go into a damned world of illusion.'

The sound of hammering echoed from above them. New beams were going into the roof of the apse.

The noise almost drowned Sankal's response, which came quietly but firmly.

'Father, I am shy person, you know it. Yet am I at maturity. Always I have many inward thoughts. Now those thoughts move like a stream to this wrong belief.' He hung his head.

Predjin stood, so that he dominated the youth. His expression was grave and sympathetic. 'Look at me, son, and do not be ashamed. All our lives are filled with such hammering as we hear now. It is the sound of an enormous material world breaking in on us. We must not heed it. This wrong belief must make you miserable.'

'Father, I have respect for your theology. But maybe what is wrong belief is right for me. No, I mean . . . Is hard to say it. To arrive at a clear belief – it's good, is it? – even if the belief is wrong. Then maybe is not wrong after all. Is instead good.'

With the merest hint of impatience, Father Predjin said, 'I don't understand your reasoning, Julius. Can we not pull out this wrong belief from your mind, like a rotten tooth?'

Sankal looked up at his mentor defiantly. He showed clenched fists, white-knuckled above the desk.

'My belief is that this island has not been maked – *made* by God. It also is an illusion, made by God's terrible adversary.'

'That's nothing more than non-belief.'

It came out defiantly: 'No, no. I believe the Evil Ones made our place where we live. Our goodness itself is an illusion. I have proof it is so.'

Thinking deeply before he replied, Father Predjin said, 'Let us suppose for an instant that we are living on an island made by these frightful beings who now possess the solar system, so that all is illusion. But yet goodness is not an illusion. Goodness is never an illusion, wherever found. Evil is the illusion . . .'

Even as he spoke, he imagined he saw something furtive and evil in the eyes of the youth standing before him.

Father Predjin studied Sankal carefully before asking, 'And have you come suddenly to your conclusion?'

'Yes. No. I realise I have always felt like this way. I just did not know it. I've always been running, have I? Only coming here – well, you gave me time for thinking. I realise the world is evil, and it gets worse. Because the Devil rules it. We always spoke of the Devil in our family. Well, now he has come in this horse-like shape to overwhelm us.'

'What is this proof you speak of?'

Sankal jumped up, to face the father angrily. 'It's in me, in the scars on my mind and on my body since I am a boy. The Devil does not have to knock to come in. He is inside already.'

After a pause, the father sat down again, and crossed himself. He said, 'You must be very unhappy to believe such a thing. That is not belief as we understand it, but sickness. Sit down, Julius, and let me tell you something. For if you seriously believe what you say, then you must leave us. Your home will be in the world of illusion.'

'I know that.' The youth looked defiant, but seated himself on a rickety chair. The hammering above continued.

'I was just discussing with someone how we were going to keep warm in the coming winter,' the father said, conversationally. 'When first I arrived on the island with two companions, we managed somehow to survive the long winter. This building was then in a terrible condition, with half the roof missing. We had no electricity and could not have afforded it had it been available.

'We burnt logs, which we chopped from fallen trees. Mannsjo was then more wooded than now it is. We lived virtually in two rooms on the ground floor. We lived off fish and little else. Occasionally, the kind people of Mannjer would skate across the ice to bring us warm clothes, bread and akavit. Otherwise, we prayed and we worked and we fasted.

'Those were happy days. God was with us. He rejoices in scarcity.

'As the years have passed, we have become more sophisticated. At first we made do with candles. Then with oil lamps and oil heaters. We are now reconnected to the electricity supply from Mannjer. Somehow it still works. Now we have to prepare for a longer darker winter, the winter of Unbelief.'

'I do not understand what you hope for,' Sankal said. 'This little piece of the past is lost somewhere outside the galaxy, where God – where your god has never been heard of.'

'They hear of him here and now.' The priest spoke very firmly. 'The so-called tourists hear of him. The so-called workers labour on his behalf. As long as the evil does not enter into us, we do the Lord's work, wherever in the universe we happen to be.'

Sankal gave a shrug. He looked over one shoulder. 'The Devil can get to you, because he owns all – every things in the world he made.'

'You will make yourself ill believing that. Such beliefs were once held by Cathars and Bogomils. They perished. What I am trying to tell you is that it is easy to mistake the danger we are in – the more than mortal danger – for the work of the Devil. There is no Devil. There is merely a desertion of God, which in itself is extremely painful in many spiritual ways. You are missing God's peace.'

From under his brows, Sankal shot Predjin a look of mischievous hatred. 'I certainly am! So I wish to leave.'

The hammering above them ceased. They heard the footsteps of the workers overhead.

Father Predjin cleared his throat. 'Julius, there is evil in men, in all of us, yes—'

Sankal's shouted interruption: 'And in the horse-devils who did such a thing in the world!'

The priest flinched but continued. 'We must regard what has happened to be part of God's strategy of free will. We can still choose between good and evil. We have the gift of life, however hard that life may be, and in it we must choose. If you go from here, you cannot come back.'

They looked at each other across the wormy old desk. Outside, beyond the round windows, a watery sun had risen from behind the eastern mountains.

'I want you to stay and help us in the struggle, Julius,' the father said. 'For your sake. We can get another baker. Another soul is a different matter.'

Again Sankal gave a cunning look askance.

'Are you afraid my hideous belief will spread among the other monks in the monastery?'

'Oh yes,' said Father Predjin. 'Yes, I am. Leprosy is contagious.'

When the youth had left, almost before his footsteps had faded from the winding wooden stair, Father Predjin hitched up his cassock and planted his knees on the worn boards of the floor. He clasped his hands together. He bowed his head.

Now there was no sound, the workmen having finished their hammering, except for a tiny flutter such as a heart might make; a butterfly flew against a window pane, unable to comprehend what held it back from freedom.

The father repeated a prayer mantra until his consciousness stilled and sank away into the depths of a greater mind. His lips ceased to move. Gradually, the scripts appeared, curling, uncurling, twisting about themselves in a three dimensional Sanskrit. There was about this lettering a sense of benediction, as if the messages conveyed were ones of good will; but in no way could the messages be interpreted, unless they were themselves the message, saying that life is a gift and an obligation, but containing a further meaning which must remain for ever elusive.

The scripts were in a colour like gold and, as they writhed and elaborated themselves, often appeared indistinct against a sandy background.

With cerebral activity almost dormant, there was no way in which intelligence could be focussed on any kind of interpretation. Nor could a finite judgement be arrived at. Labyrinthine changes taking place continually would have defied such attempts. For the scripts turned on themselves like snakes, now forming a kind of *tugra* upon the vellum of neural vacancy. Ascenders rose upwards, creating panels across which tails wavered back and forth, creating within them polychrome branches or tuft-like abstractions from twigs of amaranth.

The elaboration continued. Colour increased. Large loops created a complex motorway of lettering, and filled themselves with two contrasting arrangements of super-imposed spiral scrolls in lapis blue with carmine accents. The entanglement spread, orderly in its growth and repli-cation.

Now the entire design, which seemed to stretch infi-nitely, was either receding or pressing closer, transforming into a musical noise. That noise became more random, more like the flutter of wings against glass. As the scripts faded, as consciousness became a slowly inflowing tide, the fluttering took on a more sinister tone.

Soon – intolerably soon – breaking the mood of tran-scendent calm – the fluttering was a thundering of inscrutable nature. It was like a sound of hooves, as though a large animal was attempting clumsily to mount impossible stairs. Blundering – but brutishly set upon success.

Father Predjin came to himself. Time had passed. Cloud obscured the sky in the pupil-less eye of the round window. The butterfly lay exhausted on the sill. Still the infernal noise continued. It was as if a stallion was endeavouring to climb the wooden twisting stair from below.

He rose to his feet. 'Sankal?' he asked, in a whisper.

The father ran to the door and set his back against it, clenching the skin of his cheeks back in terror, exposing his two rows of teeth. Sweat burst like tears from his brow.

'Save me, sweet heavenly Father, save me, damn you! I'm all you've got!'

Still the great beast came on, the full power of Pentivanashenii behind it.

COGNITIVE ABILITY AND THE LIGHT BULB

The arrival of the spaceship *Conqueror* into Arcopian space proves ironic. However, it provides us with an opportunity to look back on our distant predecessors and understand something of their combative and jerry-built societies.

Once the dead bodies had been cleared from the *Conqueror*, and preserved in our museums, mechs were dispatched to examine the ship as part of our phylogenetic record.

The ship was fitted with old-fashioned quantum-computers. The *Conqueror* had left the old solar system late in 2095. It carried ten thousand human embryos in cryogenic conditions, and several million embryos, similarly frozen, of terrestrial animal genera, together with numerous plant species. There were also twenty crew, supported by anti-thanatonic drugs.

Technologists had designed the ship to accelerate to twelve per cent of the speed of light. By their computations, it was due to reach this system (where only two planets capable of supporting carbon-based life had been identified) in one hundred and ninety-six years. The power source was a fusion engine.

In those rather primitive days, attention concentrated on the hardware. It was the bacteria on the *Conqueror* which brought about disaster, killing crew and embryos alike.

Advances in radiotelescopy revealed no less than fifteen planets orbiting the Arcopia main sequence sun. At least five sustained suitable environments. In the Second Renaissance taking place in the third decade of the twenty-second century, the spiritual order of God's Exiles perfected an ion drive and equipped another interstellar ship, *Pilgrim*. *Pilgrim* was launched from Plutonian orbit in 2151. It carried with it the embryos of new species of animals, fruits and human beings. The entire journey was governed by quantors; God's Exiles did not inflict years of imprisonment on humans, as the *Conqueror* had done.

This journey took one hundred and thirty-eight years to complete. Thus the arrival was in 2289, two years before the *Conqueror* reached us, despite starting fifty-six years later.

In these improved drives we see symbols of the expansion of human consciousness. Everything is subject to change, and living things to evolutionary change, marking their passage through time. Study of the evolution of human consciousness was scarcely recognised as a discipline until interstellar flight was proved to speed conceptual processes. The necessity for understanding and dealing with totally new environments was responsible for this rapid acceleration in human mentation. A similar acceleration is recorded some forty thousand years ago in Europe, when fresh environments brought about a great expansion in the metaphors of art and sculpture – all of which represent an upward surge in cognitive ability.

Which is to say that to produce art or science is to experience a coming together of previously somewhat isolated faculties, which combine to make a greater whole. Another well-known example of such a quantal happening is the First Renaissance, a time of great advances in arts, sciences, warfare, and political management.

The twenty-second century philosopher, Almond Kunzel, has used an analogy between human consciousness and a light bulb of an old-fashioned order. Early consciousness could be likened to a forty watt bulb – sufficient dimly to illumine a room, though insufficient to study details by. The Renaissance marks a shift in brightness to sixty watts. Much more can be discerned, although illumination is not cast very far.

With the Twentieth Century, often referred to as the Savage Century, owing to its horrifying record of war, threats of war and genocide, the bulb brightens to one hundred watts. Despite the savagery, humanity is for the first time developing a form of remote awareness (remware, as we know it) to aid its exploration of all environments.

Those environments included, of course, the solar system to which our predecessors were then confined, and also the human brain. The brain was almost completely mapped by the end of the Savage Century. With the ability to genetically engineer brain function, many irregularities, caused by the jerry-building of this organism, were eradicated. Clearer thinking emerged as a result. War was obviated.

We now reached the stage of, in Kunzel's terms, the one thousand watt brain. Our offspring are born with an understanding of fractals.

This great expansion of cognitive ability led to the new perception of the universe as a series of contiguities, and to the terrestrial construction, in the year 2162, of the photon drive. The fleet of ships launched in 2200 arrived here in the planetary system of Arcopia the next year.

Our culture was thus firmly established when the old ships of 2095 and 2151 arrived, fossils of a former time. They harbour in orbits far from the planet on which humanity began — long before there was even a light bulb to light our way. Records on these gallant old hulks demonstrate how, sadly, the human world once contained less order, less joy and less fulfilment than now.

DARK SOCIETY

... for though he left this World not very many
Days past, yet every hour you know largely addeth
to that dark Society; and considering the incessant
Mortality of Mankind, you cannot conceive that
there dieth in the whole Earth so few as a thousand
an Hour ...

Sir Thomas Browne 1690

People in their millions, dead and unobliging.
Marching the clouded streets, trying still to articulate the miseries that had constricted their
previous phase of existence. Trying to articulate what had
no tongue. To recapture something ...

An undersized military computer operator in Aldershot
tapped an unimportant juridical decision into the Internet,
addressing it to a distant army outpost in a hostile country.
Like the mycelia of fungus, progressing unseen underground in a mass of branching filaments as if imbued with
consciousness, so the web of the Internet system spread
unseen across the globe, utilising even insignificant Army
ops in its blind quest for additional sustenance – and in so
doing awakening ancient chthonian forces to a resentment

of the new technology which, in its blind semi-autonomous drive for domination, threatened the forces' nutrient substrata deep in the planetary expanses of human awareness. The little op, signing over to the next shift, while those concealed forces were already – in a way that took no heed of time or human reason – moving, moving to re-establish themselves in the non-astronomical universe, checked with the clock and betook himself to the nearest chipper.

The battalion had commandeered an old manor house for the duration of the campaign. Other ranks were housed in huts in the grounds, well inside the fortified perimeter. Only officers were comfortably housed in the big, old house.

Year by year they were destroying the mansion, pulling down the oak panelling for fires, using the library for an indoor shooting gallery, misusing anything vulnerable.

The colonel damped the audio on his power box and turned to his adjutant.

'You heard most of that, Julian? Division sitrep from Aldershot. Verdict of the court martial just in. They've found our Corporal Cleat mentally unstable, unfit to stand trial.'

'Dismissed the service?'

'Exactly. Just as well. Saves any publicity. See to his discharge papers, will you?'

The adjutant stalked towards the door and called the orderly sergeant.

The colonel went over to the wood fire burning in the grate and warmed his behind. He stared out of the tall window at the manor grounds. A morning haze limited visibility to about two hundred yards. Everything looked peaceful enough. A group of soldiers on fatigues were strengthening the security fence. The tall trees of the drive were in themselves a reassurance of stability. Yet it never did to forget that this was enemy territory.

He failed to understand the case of Corporal Cleat. Certainly the man was strange. It happened that the colonel knew the Cleat family. The Cleats had made a great deal of money in the early eighties, trading in a chain of electronic stores, which they had sold off at great profit to a German company. Cleat should have become an officer; instead he had chosen to serve in the ranks.

Some quarrel with his father, silly bugger. Very English habit. Went and married a Jewish girl. Of course, Vivian Cleat, the father, had been a bit of a tight-arse and no mistake. Got himself knighted for all that.

It was useless to try to understand other people. The Army's concern was with ordering people, getting them organised, not understanding them. Order was everything, when you thought about it.

All the same, Corporal Cleat had been guilty. The whole battalion knew that. Division had handled the matter well, for once; the less publicity the better, at a rather tricky time. Discharge Cleat and forget about the whole business. Get on with the damned war.

'Julian?'

'Yessir?'

'What did you make of Corporal Cleat? Arrogant little bugger, wouldn't you say? Headstrong?'

'Couldn't say, sir. Wrote poetry, so I'm informed.'

'Better get in touch with his wife. Lay on transport for her to meet Cleat and get the man off our hands. Goodbye to bad rubbish.'

'Sir, the wife died while Cleat was in the glasshouse. Eunice Rosemary Cleat, age twenty-nine. You may recall her father was a herpetologist at Kew. Lived out near Esher somewhere. A verdict of suicide was brought in.'

'On him?'

'On her.'

'Oh, bugger. Well, ring Welfare. Get shot of the man. Get him off our hands. Back to England.'

He took a passage on a ferry. He huddled in a corner of the passenger deck, arms wrapped round himself, fearful of air and motion and he knew not what. On the dock, he bought a pasty and ate it, sheltering from the rain. He thumbed a lift which took him all the way to Cheltenham. From there he paid for a seat on a coach to Oxford. He needed money, lodgings. He also needed some form of help. Mental aid. Rehabilitation. He did not know exactly what he wanted. Only that something was wrong, that he was not himself.

At Oxford, he booked into a cheap hotel in the Iffley Road. In the market, he sought out a cheap Indian clothing stall where he bought himself a T-shirt, a pair of stone-washed jeans, and a heavy-duty Chinese-made over-shirt. He went to see his bank in Cornmarket. In one of his accounts, a substantial sum of money remained.

He got drunk that night with a friendly mob of young men and women. In the morning he could remember none of their names. He was sick, and left the cheap hotel in a bad temper. As he quit the room, he looked back hastily. Someone or something had caught his eye. He thought a man was sitting dejectedly on the unmade bed. There was no one. Another delusion.

He went to his old college to see the bursar. It was out of term time; behind the worn, grey walls of Septuagint, life had congealed like cold mutton gravy. The porter informed him that Mr Robbins was away for the morning, looking over some property in Wolvercote. He sat in Robbins' office, huddled in a corner, hoping not to be seen. Robbins did not return until three thirty in the afternoon.

Robbins ordered a pot of tea. 'As you know, Ozzie, your "flat" is really a storeroom, and has reverted to that use. It's been – what? Four years?'

'Five.'

'Well, it's a bit awkward.' He looked considerably annoyed. 'More than a bit, in fact. Look, Ozzie, I have a pile of work to do. I suppose we could put you up at home, just for a—'

'I don't want that. I want my old room back. Want to hide away, out of everyone's sight. Come on, John, you owe me a favour.'

Robbins said, calmly pouring Earl Grey into his cup, 'I owe you bloody nothing, my friend. It was your father who was the college benefactor. Mary and I have done enough for you as it is. Besides, we know what you've been up to, blotting your service career. To put you up here in college again is to break all the rules. As you know.'

'Sod you, then!' He turned away in anger. But as he reached the door, Robbins called him back.

The storeroom under the eaves of Joshua Building looked much as it had done when it had served as Cleat's flat. Light filtered in from one northern skylight. It was a long room, one side of it sloping sharply with the angle of the roof, as if a giant had taken a butcher's knife to it. The place smelt closed, musty with ancient knowledge percolating up from below.

Cleat stood staring angrily at a pile of old armchairs for a while. Setting to work dragging them to one side, he found his bed was still there, and even his old oak chest, which he had had since schooldays. He knelt on the dusty boards and unlocked it.

The chest contained a few possessions. Clothes, books, a Japanese aviator's sword, no drink. An unframed photograph of Eunice wearing a scarf. He slammed the lid down and fell back on the bed.

Holding the photograph up to the light, he studied the coloured representation of Eunice's face. Pretty, yes; rather silly, yes. But no more of a fool than he. Love had been a torture, merely emphasising his own futility. You took more note of a woman than a man, of course. You expected nothing from your fellow men – or your bloody father. All those signals women put out, unknowingly, designed to grab your attention . . .

Human physiology and psychology had been cunningly designed for maximum human disquiet, he thought.

Small wonder he had made a miniature hell of his life.

Later he went out into town and got drunk, ascending from Morrell's ales through vodka to a cheap whiskey in a Jerico pub.

Next morning was bad. Shakily, he climbed on the bed to stare out of the skylight. The world seemed to have been drained of colour overnight. The slate roofs of Septuagint shone with damp. Beyond, slate roofs of other distant colleges, an entire landscape of slate and tile, with abysses between sharp-peaked hills.

After a while, he gathered himself together, put on his shoes, and went along the attic corridor before descending the three flights of Number Twelve staircase. The stone steps were worn from centuries of students who had been installed in rooms here, each in a little cell with an oak door, to sup up what learning they could. The wooden panelling on the walls was kicked and scuffed. How like prison, he thought.

Down in the inner quad, he looked about him be-musedly. The Fellows Hall stood to one side. On impulse, he crossed the flagstones and went in. The hall was built in a Perpendicular style, with tall windows and heavy linen-fold panels. Between the windows hung solemn portraits of past benefactors. His father's portrait had been removed from near the end of the line; in its stead hung the portrait of a Japanese man in gown and mortar board, gazing serenely through his spectacles.

A scout had been polishing silver trophies in one corner of the room. He came forward now, to ask, with a mixture of obsequiousness and sharpness which Cleat remembered in college servants, 'Can I help you, sir? This is the Fellows' Hall.'

'Where's the portrait of Sir Vivian Cleat which used to hang here?'

'This is Mr Yashimoto, sir. One of our recent benefactors.'

'I know it's Mr Yashimoto. I'm asking you about another eminent benefactor, Vivian Cleat. It used to hang here. Where is it?'

'I expect it's gone, sir.'

'Where, man? Where's it gone?'

The scout was tall and thin and dry of countenance. As if to squeeze one last drop of moisture from his face, he frowned and said, 'There's the Buttery, sir. Some of our less important worthies were moved there last Hilary Term, as I recall.'

Outside the Buttery, he ran into Homer Jenkins, a one-time friend who held the Hughenden Chair in Human Relations. Jenkins had been a sportsman in his time, a rowing blue, and retained a slim figure into his sixties. A Leander scarf was draped round his neck, a reminder of past glories. Jenkins agreed blithely that Cleat's father's portrait now hung behind the bar in the Buttery.

'Why isn't it with the other college benefactors?'

'You don't really want me to answer that one, do you, dear boy?' Uttered with a smile and head slightly on one side. Cleat remembered the Oxford style.

'Not greatly.'

'Very wise. If I may say so, it's a surprise to see you about here again.'

'Thanks so much.' As he turned on his heel, the Hughenden professor called, 'Hard lines about Eunice, Ozzie, dear boy!'

He bought a bowl of soup in a Pizza Piazza, feeling ill, telling himself he was no longer in prison. But the narrative of his life had in some way been mislaid and something like an intestinal rumbling told him that there was within himself a part he would never know again. *Unseen, the cancer stops to lick chops and then again devours . . .* A line from a poem by – whom? As if it mattered.

A teenage girl drifted into the wine bar and said, 'Oh, there you are. I thought I might find you lurking here.' She was studying Jurisprudence at Lady Margaret Hall, she said, and finding it all a bit of a bore. But Daddy was a judge, and so . . . She sighed and laughed simultaneously.

As she talked, he realised she had been one of the group

of students from the previous night. He had taken no notice of her that he could recall.

'I could tell you were a follower of Chomsky,' she said, laughing.

'I believe in nothing.' To himself he thought, sickly, but I must believe in something or other, if only I could get at it.

'You look well-ghastly today, if you'll forgive my saying so. But then, you're a poet, aren't you? You were spouting Seamus Heeley last night.'

'It's *Heaney*, Seamus Heaney, or so I'm led to believe. Do you want a drink?'

'You're a poet and a criminal, so you said!' Laughingly, she clutched his arm. 'Or was it a criminal and a poet? Which came first, the chicken or the egg?'

He did not want her, did not need her company, but there she stood, new minted, eager, unenslaved, spring-like, waifish, agog for life.

'Want to come back to my dreadful dump for coffee?'

'Depends. How dreadful?' Still half-laughing, teasing, bright, curious, trusting, yet with a little something like guile, born for a relationship such as this.

'*Historically* dreadful.'

'Okay. Coffee and research. Nothing more.'

Later, he told himself, she had wanted something more. Half wanted at least, or she would never have made her way before him in her brief skirt, upwards round the labyrinthine coils of Staircase Twelve to that lumber room, or have fallen, when she gained the top, panting and laughing with open mouth − pristine as the inside of a tulip − on the dusty bed. He had not meant to rush her. Not meant that at all.

Well, she was a sporting young lady, perhaps aware afterwards that she had unconsciously enticed him, an older
world-stained man with a smell of incarceration yet about
him, and had departed without indecent haste, still with a
kind of smile, a smile now more like a sneer, towards safety
or ruination as character dictated. Degraded, defeated possibly, but full of a spirit – he forced himself to hope – which
would not admit to that defeat. Not like Eunice.

'Whatever drives us to these things . . .' he said, half
aloud, but did not complete the sentence, aware of his
treachery even to himself.

Near at hand, a relay clicked.

The sky darkened over Oxford. The rain came down again
as if the hydrological cycle were working out a new means
of replenishing the Thames from an untapped level in the
troposphere. It washed against the lumber room windows
with antediluvian splendour.

Towards evening he stirred himself and ventured further into the recesses of the room. There he discovered a
crate full of his old books and videos. Pulling it out he
found, hiding further in the gloom, a box containing his
old computer.

Without particularly conscious volition, he carried the
Power Paq from its box and plugged it in to the mains. He
dusted off the monitor screen with his sock. LCDs winked
at him.

He pushed in a CD protruding like a tongue and rifled
the keys with his fingers. He had forgotten how to operate
the thing.

A leering face came on, moving into close-up from a red
distance. He managed to remove it and eject the disc,
whereupon a slight whirring started and a sheet of A4

paper began extruding from the fax slot. He regarded it in nervous surprise as it floated to the floor. He switched off the computer.

In a minute, he picked up the message and sat on the bed to read it. The sender of the fax addressed him by his first name. The text was only partly comprehensible:

Oz as was Oz,

If I say I know where you are. Physical action. Its low comedy marks us, but such. It is such. Where there are no placed no place no position at all as regarding bakers' shops.

Or to say only to say or to say all the more the more there is to say like stamens on the pyracanthus. Is yours also? Also an ingredient. I hope it comes through. Trying.

Clear the street. Clearer in the street. The crooked way. I mean the clear the path from. You and I. For ever its.

The existence. Can you speak of existence of what does not existence. I clear nonexistence. I nonexist. Speak.

Speak me. New street no clear street clear communicate. Slow. Difficulty.

Past tense.

Eunice

'Bloody nonsense,' he said, screwing up the paper, determined not to show himself he was disturbed by the mere fact of the message. A haunted computer? Rubbish, balls, idiocy. Someone was trying to make a fool of him; one of the fellows of the college, most like.

A peremptory knock at the door.

'Come.'

Homer Jenkins entered the lumber room, catching Cleat standing there in the middle of the room. Cleat threw the ball of paper at him. Jenkins caught it neatly.

'Evenings are closing in.'

'The rain should clear.'

'At least it's mild. Don't you need a light in here?'

Polite North European noises. Jenkins came to the point. 'A young woman has invaded the porter's lodge with a complaint against you. Sexual molestation, that kind of thing. I am quite able to deal with young women of her kind, but I must warn you the Bursar says that if there is such an occurrence again, we shall have to rethink your position, doubtless to your detriment.'

Cleat stood his ground.

'That study of yours on the Spanish Civil War, Homer. Have you completed it yet? Is it published, or are you still stuck on that bit where Franco became Governor of the Canary Islands?'

Jenkins was fully Cleat's equal when it came to standing one's ground. The Jenkins family had enjoyed wealth for several generations, ever since the days of Jenkins' Irresistible Flea Powder (no longer mentioned by the newer generations). They owned rolling acres on the Somerset border. Foxhunting went on there, and archery. This background made Homer Jenkins confident when it came to standing his own ground. He did it, moreover, with a kind of smile and an outward thrust of the chin.

In a calm voice, he said, 'Ozzie, you received some recognition as a poet before you served your stretch in clink, and of course the college welcomed your success, minor though it was. We attempted to overlook your other proclivities *vis-à-vis* your father's endowment to Septuagint.

'However, if you wish to get back on your feet again, and restore if possible your reputation, you must be advised that the college's benevolence extends only so far. Retribution is never pleasant.'

Turning with calm dignity, he made for the door.

'You sound like Hamlet's father!' Cleat shouted. Jenkins did not turn back.

He woke on the following morning to a faint click, audible even above the sound of rain on the roof just over his bed. Another note was emerging from the fax.

Oz was,
    O Im getting the it of hanging hang of it. Soon
soon hobnails on streets I speak you ordinary.
Difficulty. Garble garble other physical laws. Lores
    Follow me ill repeat it follow.
    Follow dont keep still. Still love you still. Still or
moving.
    Eunice

He sat with the flimsy paper in his hand, thinking about his late wife. A fragment of a poem came to his head.

> *Being among the men taken captive*
> *The men the enemy humiliated*
> *The men who cursed themselves*
> *The men whose beloved women had*
> *Preceded them to hell*

He began to conjure up a long poem where a man, captive like himself, suffered all to be reunited with a dead wife, even if it entailed a descent into hell itself. He thrilled to the vision. Perhaps he could write again. Words and phrases jostled in his mind like prisoners seeking release.

This time, he did not screw up the message. Without necessarily giving it credence, he nevertheless felt belief of some kind stir within him – a remarkable phenomenon in itself.

Yes, yes, he would write and confound them all. He still had – whatever he once had. Except Eunice. For her he felt an unexpected longing, but he set it aside under the prompting to write. He rummaged about in his chest, but found no suitable writing materials. A journey down to the nearest stationer was indicated. An image swam before his eyes, not of his dead wife, but of a mint, unblemished pack of white A4 copy paper.

Locking the door of his room behind him, he stood for a moment in the gloom of the landing. Waves of uncertainty overcame him like a personalised nausea. Was he any good as a poet? He had been no good as a soldier. Or a son. Or even as a husband.

He would bloody well show the likes of Homer Jenkins, if he had to go through hell to do so. But the gloom, the airlessness of this top landing was oppressive . . .

He went slowly down the first flight of stairs. The rain was falling even more heavily now, making an intense drumming. The further down the stairs he went, the darker it became.

Pausing at one landing, he peered out of a slit-like window into the quad below. So heavy was the downpour, it was hard to distinguish anything clearly, beyond walls of stone inset with blind windows. A flash of lightning came, to reveal a fleeing figure far below, carrying what looked like a plate – it could not be a halo! – over his head. Another flash. Cleat had a momentary impression that the whole college was sinking, sliding down intact into the clayey soils of Oxford, where bones of gigantic reptiles lay yet undiscovered.

Sighing, he continued downwards.

A little fat man, fortyish and sallow, with rain dripping from his hair and blunt face, bumped into Cleat at the next stairwell.

'What a soaker, eh? They told me you were back, Ozzie,' he said, without any great display of delight. 'There's one of your metaphysical poems I've always rather liked. The one about, oh, you know – how does it go?'

Cleat did not recognise the man. 'Sorry, it's been—'

'Something about first causes. Ashes and strawberries, I seem to remember. You see, the way we scientists look at it is that before the Big Bang, the *ylem* existed nowhere. It had nowhere to exist *in*. At all at all, as our Irish friends purportedly say with some frequency. The elementary particles released in the initial – you understand *explosion* is hardly an adequate word – perhaps you poets can come up with a better one – *ylem*'s a good one – the initial bang included in its bargain bundle both time and space. So that in that first one-hundredth of a second—'

His eyes blurred with intellectual excitement. A small bubble of spit formed on his lower lip like a new universe coming into being. He had begun to wave his arms, when Cleat protested that he did not want to be drawn into a discussion at that moment.

'Of course not,' said the scientist, laughing, and clutching Cleat's shirt so that he would not escape. 'Mind you, we all feel the same.'

'We don't. We couldn't possibly.'

'We do, we cannot grasp that initial concept of nothingness, of a place without dimensions of space or time. So *nothingy* that even nothing cannot exist.' He laughed in a panting sort of way, like an intelligent bull terrier. 'The concept frightens the hell out of me – such a no-place must be either bliss or perpetual torment. It is the task of science to make clear what previously was—'

Cleat cried out that he had an appointment below, but the grip on his shirt did not slacken.

'Where science appears to meet religion. This timeless, spaceless space – the pre-*ylem* universe, so to speak – bears more than a superficial resemblance to Heaven, the old Christian myth. Heaven may still be around, permeated, of course, by fossil radiation—'

The scientist interrupted himself by bursting into laughter, pressing his face nearer to Cleat's.

'Or of course – you'll appreciate this, Ozzie, being a poet – equally, *Hell*! "This is Hell, nor are we out of it . . .", as Shakespeare immortally puts it.'

'*Marlowe!*' screamed Cleat. Tearing himself away from the other's grasp, he rushed off, down the next flight of steps.

'Tut, of course, Marlowe . . .' said the scientist, standing alone and lonely on the stair. 'Marlowe. Must remember. Good old Christopher Marlowe.'

He mopped his streaming brow with a used tissue.

But it was getting so dark. The noise grew louder. The stairs turned about anti-clockwise in tortuous lapidity, and with them went Cleat's grip on reality. It was a relief when the steps terminated and he came to a broader space, marked at each end by archways, beyond which dim lanterns glowed in the darkness.

He was slightly puzzled. Somehow, he seemed to have overshot ground level. The clamminess of the air certainly indicated he was underground, lost in the ample cellarage of Septuagint. He remembered the cellarage of old; here, no dusty racks of bottles were to be seen. The halitus of his breath hung in the air, slow to disperse.

Going forward hesitantly, he passed under one of the arches into a cobbled space, where more steps presented themselves. He looked up. Everything was hard to make out. He could not determine whether rock or stone or sky was overhead. No rain fell. He found it uncanny that the downpour could have cut off. Something prompted him not to call out. There was nothing for it but to go forward.

His mood was glum. Not for the first time, he was on bad terms with himself. Why was it he could not establish friendly relationships with others? Why be so unpleasant to the fat scientist – Neil Someone, could it have been? – who was, when all was said and done, no more eccentric than many other dons in the University of Oxford.

Oxford? This could not be Oxford, or even Cowley! He plodded on until, uncertain of his whereabouts, he paused. Immediately, a figure – Cleat could not tell if it was male or female – was passing by, grey of aspect and clad in a long gown.

'Have you seen a stationer near here?'

The figure paused, tweaked up his cheeks in the genesis of a smile, then strode on. As Cleat started off again, the figure vanished – there, then not there.

'Shit and *ylem*, very peculiar,' he said, hiding a distinct sense of unease from himself. Vanished, completely vanished, like one of Neil Someone's elementary particles . . .

The steps broadened, became shallow, petered out into cobbles. On either side stood what passed, he supposed, for houses; they contained no signs of life. It was all very old-fashioned in an artificial way, like a nineteenth-century representation of sixteenth-century Nuremburg.

He continued uncertainly to descend once more until he came to a wide space which he mentally termed the Square. Here he halted.

As soon as he stopped, the surroundings began moving. He took a pace back in startlement: everything stopped. He stopped: buildings, roadways, broke into uneasy movement. He took another pace: everything stopped. He stopped again: everything he could see, the dim and watercolour environs about him, launched into movement again. A sort of forward but circular movement.

An image came to him of a crab, the crab who believes that everyone but he walks sideways.

This relativity of movement was the least of it. For when he walked, not only was the universe stilled, but it was empty of people (people?). But when he stood still, not only did the universe begin its crabwise shuffle, but it became the stage for a bustling crowd of people (people?).

Cleat thought longingly of his safe army prison cell.

Remaining stock still, he attempted to single out faces in the crowd. To his mortal eyes, how dead and unobliging they were! Jostle they certainly did, pushing past him and past each other, not hurriedly but merely because there seemed so little room: although, with the constant movement of streets and thoroughfares, the various ways seemed to be expanding at a steady rate to accommodate them. Their clothes lacked colour and variety.

It was hard to distinguish male from female. Their contours, their faces, body languages, were somehow blurred. He found by experiment that by keeping his head rigid and allowing his eyes to slide out of focus he could in fact make out individual faces: man, woman, young, old, dark, light, occidental, oriental, long-haired, short-haired, bearded or otherwise, moustachioed or otherwise, tall, thin, stocky, fat, upright or stooped. Yet – what was wrong with his retina? – all alike without expression; not merely without expression, but seemingly without the facility to conjure up expressions. Abstracts of faces.

Surrounding him on all sides was an immense dark society, who appeared neither alive nor dead. And this society was proceeding this way and that, entirely without ambition or objective.

They were like phantasms. Chillingly silent.

They jostled by Cleat until he could stand the tension no more. As he began to run, as he first tensed his leg muscles for flight, the vast homogeneous crowd vanished, was gone in an instant, leaving him isolated in a motion-less street.

'There must be a scientific explanation,' he said. The only one that occurred to him was that he was suffering a kind of terminal delusion. He shook his head violently, trying to think himself back into the familiar old expand-ing universe of hurtling velocities to which he was accustomed. But this present cloudy world remained, obeying its own variant set of physical laws.

What had Eunice's second message said? Wasn't that something about other physical laws?

A cold horror gripped him, drying his throat, chilling his skin.

Bracing himself to proceed, he told himself that what-ever was happening, he deserved what he got.

He walked and walked, to emerge at last before a dif-ferent kind of building; an attempt, he thought, at some kind of a . . . well, town hall? It conformed to no order of architecture he knew, being built of a spongy material, with elaborate flights of steps leading to no visible doorway, with balconies to which no access was visible, with towering columns supporting no visible roofing, with a portico under which no one could walk. It was preposterous, impossible and imposing.

He stopped in some wonderment – though wonderment was a quality of which he was rapidly being drained.

Immediately he stopped, the universe was set in motion and the enormous building bore down on him like an ocean liner on a helpless swimmer.

He remained rooted to the spot and thus found himself entering the great structure.

A brighter light than he had hitherto encountered in the cloudy world illuminated the inside of the hall. He was at a loss to think where it came from.

Scattered about the floor were huge piles of belongings, extremely tatterdemalion in aspect. Cloudy personages were picking through the heaps. Everything moved with that unsettling crabwise movement, as if caught in the whirlpool of a spiral nebula.

If he stood stock still, he could see what was happening. He found he could relax his auditory nerve much like his optical one, and so was able to hear sounds for the first time. The voices of the personages drifted to him, high and squeaky, as if they had inhaled helium. They seemed to be exclaiming with delight as they disinterred items from the heaps.

He moved forward to see more closely. Everything vanished. He halted. It all returned. *No, I don't want this . . .* But when he shook his head involuntarily, the building became no more than an echoing empty place, moving with the stealth of a cat.

The various heaps consisted of curious old belongings. Mountains of old suitcases, many battered and worn as if humanly exhausted from a long, sad journey. Stacks and stacks of footwear of all kinds: lace-up boots, ladies' slippers, clodhoppers, children's patent leather shoes, bedroom slippers, brogues, shoes for this, shoes for that, worn or new, shoes enough to walk to Mars and back by themselves.

Eyeglasses in as large a glassy heap, pince-nez, horn-rims, monocles, all the rest of them. Clothes: countless rags of every description indescribable, towering up towards the roof. And – no, yes – hair! Hair by the tonne, glossy black, lily white, all shades in between, hair of humans, curled and bobbed and straight, some scalps with pigtails, their ribbons still trailing. Teeth, too, the most terrible pile of all, molars, wisdoms, dog teeth, eye teeth, even milk teeth, some with flesh adhering to their forked roots.

They vanished. Instinctively, Cleat had moved, shaken by an agonising sense of recognition.

He fell to the ground, remaining kneeling. The dreadful interior came back.

Now he saw more clearly, by unfocussing his eyes, the people who picked over the sordid array. They merely reclaimed what had once been theirs, what remained rightfully theirs.

He saw women – yes, that's it, bald women of all ages – reclaiming their hair, trying it on, being made whole again.

Many others of the dark society stood by, applauding, as the seekers were made whole.

Then he thought he saw Eunice.

Of course, she had Jewish blood in her veins. Here in this terrible place you might find her, among the wronged, the disinherited, the slaughtered.

He crouched where he was, not daring to move in case

she vanished. Was it she? A watercolour version of the Eunice he had once loved?

Something like tears moved upwards through his being, a gigantic remorse for mankind. He cried her name.

Everything vanished except the great empty hall, unmoving as fate.

He froze, and she was approaching him!

She held out a hand in recognition.

Even as he reached for it, she vanished.

When he froze into stillness, she and all about her faded back into being.

'We can never be together,' she said, and her voice carried a distant and forlorn note, like an owl's cry above sodden woodland. 'For one of us is of the dead and one is not, my Ozzie dearest!'

She kept fading in and out as he tried to reply.

She knelt beside him, resting a hand on his shoulder. They remained like that in silence, heads close together, the man, the woman. He learnt to speak with almost no lip movement.

'I don't understand.'

'I never understood . . . But my messages reached you. You have come! Even here you have come! How brave you are.'

At her whispered words, a little warmth kindled within him: so he had after all some virtue, something on which to build in future, whatever that future was to be . . . He stared into her eyes but saw no response there, indeed found a difficulty in appreciating them as eyes.

Brokenly, he said, 'Eunice, if it is you in any way, I'm *sorry* – just deeply and unremittingly sorry. For everything. I'm living in a hell of my own. I came to say that, to tell you that, to follow you down into Gehenna.'

It seemed she regarded him steadily. He knew she saw him not as once she had but now as a kind of thing, an anomaly in whatever served here as a variant on the space-time continuum.

'All these . . .' As he almost gestured, the enormous sordid piles wavered towards invisibility. 'What are they doing *now*? It's . . . I mean, the Holocaust, it's all so long ago. So *long* . . .'

She was disinclined to answer until he prompted her, when her being swam and almost disintegrated before his eyes.

'There is no *now* here, no *long ago*. Can you understand that? It's not like that here. Those time indicators are arbitrary rules in your . . . whatever – dimensions? Here, they have no meaning.'

He moaned, covering his eyes against an overpowering sense of loss.

When he peeped between his fingers, the building was again in motion. He remained rigid – thinking, if there's no *now* here, neither is there a proper *here* – and passed through the walls into a kind of space that was not a space. He thought he had lost Eunice, but the general movement carried her close again, still kneeling towards him.

She was speaking, explaining, as if to her there had been no sense of absence.

'Nor is there any name, once passionately spoken but long-forgotten in your time-afflicted sphere, which is not tenanted here. All, even the most maligned, must join this vast society, increasing its number day by day.' Was she singing? Was he hearing aright in his state of profound disturbance? Was it even possible they communicated at all?

'The myriads who have left no memorial behind, and those whose reputations linger through what you term *ages* – all find their place . . .'

Her voice faded as he moved imploringly, hoping for a more human word. If he could get her back . . . But the thought dislocated as again the great hall was empty and still, filled only with an immense silence as austere as death itself.

Again he was forced to crouch, immobile, until the semblances of habitation and her smudgy presence re-entered the cloudy world.

The shade of Eunice continued to talk, perhaps unaware that anything had happened – or maybe that he had vanished from her variety of sight.

'. . . King Harold is here, removing the arrow from his eye; Sophocles, recovered from his hemlock; whole armies freed of their wounds; the Bogomils, back again; Robespierre undecapitated; Archbishop Cranmer and his brave speech absolved from the flames; Julius Caesar, unstabbed; Cleopatra herself, unharmed by asps, as I by my father's cobra. You must learn, Ozzie . . .'

As she droned on with her long, long list, as if she had for ever in which to specify a myriad individuals – and so she has, he thought in dismay – he could only ask himself, over and over, how do I get back to Oxford, how can I ever get back to Septuagint, with or without this phantasm of my love?

'. . . Magdeburg, Mohacs, Lepanto, Stalingrad, Kosovo, Saipan, Kohima, Agincourt, Austerlitz, Okinawa, Somme, Geok-Depe, the Boyne, Crécy . . .'

And will this shade assist me?

He broke into her litany.

Scarcely moving his lips, he asked, 'Eunice, Eunice, my

poor ghost, I fear you. I fear everything hereabouts. I knew Hell would be dreadful, but not that it would be at all like this. How can I return with you to the real world? Tell me please.'

The hall was still marvellously in movement, as though its substance was music rather than stone. Now she was more distant from him, and her reply, dreadful as it was, came thin and piping, watery as bird song, so that at first he could hardly believe he had heard her correctly.

'No, no, my precious. You are mistaken, as you always have been.'

'Yes, yes, but—'

'This is *Heaven* we are in. Hell is where you came from, my precious one, Hell with all its punishing physical conditions! This is Heaven.'

He collapsed motionless on his face, and once again the great hall with all its restitutions went about its grand harmonious movements.

GALAXY ZEE

AUTUMN. Autumn had come to Galaxy Zee. On a million million uninhabited planets, trees of all varieties turned their backs to a freshening wind and shed leaves like sepia tears. On a million million inhabited planets, where trees were permitted, there too those trees which lived their lives out in the stony solitude of streets, sent their browned tears bowling down the highways to Distribution Centres. In those centres they would be machine-masticated into nourishment for the huddled poor. The huddled poor would struggle to comfort themselves against the new chill in a million million atmospheres.

TERRAFORMING. Where could they run to, these paupers? Not to another planet. Planet A resembled Planet B resembled Planet C resembled Planet D, right through a million million alphabets. All planets had been terraformed alike. All lifestyles were alike. All valleys had been filled by levelled mountains, all mountains had been made low. And those who lived on a billion billiard ball worlds were alike in skin colour, the perfect tintless, odourless, wrinkleless skin that with its million million miles of texture covered all the inhabitants of Galaxy Zee.

THE POOR. The poor had no regret that they were poor. There were millions upon millions like them, identical with them. They were programmed to be poor throughout life. Never did they lift their eyes to wealth or warmth. The Great Programme made no allowance for mercy. Winters were programmed to follow summers on the million million planets of Galaxy Zee. Winters were programmed to winnow the poor. Frosts glittered in the air, winds rushed like great brooms through the thoroughfares, flesh became chill to the touch. It was a time to die, to join the great blackness of night. By the end of winter, hundreds of millions of the poor would no longer infest the mean streets at the backs of cities. Nothing was left to chance: everything was programmed. Except that this much was left to chance: that the man sheltering in Doorway X would survive, whereas his next door neighbour sheltering in Doorway Y would expire. Such minor statistical randomness was not important. The death mattered no more than the life.

THE RICH. It was the poor who had nothing to do. The Rich were always busy. In darkened rooms, members of the Rich consulted therapists on the question of why they had so much to do. The healthier ones joined clubs where they were likely to kill one another. Most of their days were filled with very important meetings and consultations. They flew from one identical city to the next identical city to speak or to listen, or to report on those who spoke or listened. Sometimes while they were meeting, their cities fell apart like broken hearts. They funded or arranged or attended great banquets. At these banquets, serious men and women rose and spoke on such topics of the day as 'Why Are The Poor So Many?' and 'Why Are The Poor Determined To Remain Poor?' and 'Should Hunting Hengiss Be Made Less Dangerous?'

THE HENGISS. No actual animals survived on any of the million million planets of Galaxy Zee. The hengiss was a manufacture. Since the hengiss was made of stellena, a steel-plastic material containing its own human DNA genome-strain, it was regarded as animal and, in fact, resembled the front part of a clawed horse with two legs. It fed on mutantin. Throughout the course of ten days, a hengiss was fed and exercised and carefully tortured, to improve its temperament.

THE HUNT. Every ten days, a hunt was held in every city. At the start of the hunt, uniformity prevailed. The current hengiss was taken to the centre of the main square, the same in every city, and at the same time released. Off went the hengiss, running furiously, seeking escape. It was unprogrammed. This was the great crime. Its movements could not be predicted. However, it was essential that its end was predictable. Off went the Rich in pursuit, all clad in motiles making great noise, speeding, speeding, clashing one against the other, sparking, sparking, swerving and jarring in pursuit.

THE VICTORS. Ahead rushed the great hengiss. It would leave the streets to swarm up the side of a building, a great building whose walls swelled and burned as the Hengiss climbed. Through windows, burning, blazing, blasting its course through rooms, doors, walls and windows. The motiles rose like a swarm of hornets to pursue. Many crashed. Others in sagacious pursuit closed on the fleeing animal. Dive as it might, and run inexhaustibly, still the hengiss was overtaken – until in desperation it turned at bay. Then the nearest Rich threw themselves upon it and bludgeoned it to extinction with nuclear prods. A banquet for the victors followed.

THE UNICRAT. Stationed in higher dimensions was the Unicrat, the Maker of Worlds. These dimensions were multiple, mirroring each other, sometimes multiplying, sometimes diminishing. They diminished until the Maker of Worlds would be the size of a pinhead, had size existed as a factor. Or they swelled like a nuclear cloud until the Maker of Worlds was Itself greater than the universe It controlled – had such dimensions utilised the factor of size.

These dimensions had been purged of size and of time. Eternity did not exist, nor did time: there was only an etiolated Nowness.

The Unicrat Itself spanned dimensions.

Under one of Its mandibles on Its left flank lay an alectrollic reduction of Galaxy Zee. The mandible ran its sensor over the reduction, which resembled in some respects a gigantic camera obscura, in which suns and planets moved according to rigid physical law – and living beings with them.

The Unicrat's factual part spoke to Its judgemental part in the language of light-impulse It used for self-meditation.

'My plan is not working out properly.'

Judgemental replied. 'Uniformity has triumphed. The physical laws have been drawn up too tightly.'

'They have some randomness.'

'Not enough.'

'I see that man in Doorway X survives, whereas the man in Doorway Y dies. That is random.'

'Just that effect applies in all cities on all million million planets of Galaxy Zee.'

'Is action to be taken?'

The judgemental replied, 'Many eons ago, we sent down a Son to enliven matters and bring fresh thinking. The same experiment might be attempted again.'

'Yes. But can we hope for better success? I feel the plan should be scrapped.'

'Quite. But a last chance . . .'

THE SON. All at precisely the same time, ignoring light years, the Unicrat's sons materialised on each of the million million planets of Galaxy Zee. The Son was made largely of impervium. Its face was a benevolent and immoveable mask, its heart, unmoving, sent out electric impulses. It strode first among the poor, who feared it and cowered away from it. Still they did not flee, hoping for some possible free benefit.

'Do not despair. One day the galaxy will be yours and you will own it.' Thus spoke the Son to the poor. To which the shouted response was 'Rubbish!'

'Your children are so thin. Yet they are beautiful. Suffer them to come to me.' To which the shouted response was 'Paedophile!'

'What can I do to help you?' To which the shouted response was 'Kill the Rich!'

'You miserable wretches!' said the Son in contempt.

THE TRAP. When the Son went to the quarters where the Rich lived, he found a fat and evil-faced man planning a trap to kill his rival. The fifteenth floor of his palace he had entirely filled to a depth of twenty feet with various slimes and bloods and shredded bones of the recently dead. On the fourteenth floor, a banquet was spread, to which the hated rival was invited. When the rival was seated, it needed but the pressure on a button and all the filth in the floor above would come flooding down and drown him.

The Son said to this fat man, 'I am seeking some mercy somewhere here. Will you not forgive your rival and thus save your world?'

'It is predetermined he will die,' said the fat man. 'I consulted a psycho-necessiter and it said my rival will die today. So I can't stop the process, not even to save this world.'

The rival came, wary, bold, sly. He confronted the heavily laid banqueting table and perceived that the fruit piled there was plastic. A quick covert infra-red search revealed the vital button. Seizing his fat enemy, he plunged his thumb on the button. The ceiling burst open. Down came the rancid flood. Both men were drowned, clutching each other in hatred.

The Son decided there was no remedy for this world.

All the Sons decided there was no remedy for their world.

DESTRUCTION. The work of destruction was promptly begun. Crevices like burning red mouths appeared, tearing apart the mantle of the planets as if it were so much cloth. Into these gulfs plunged the hengiss, escaping at last, only to be at once consumed. Small things like shoes scuttled forth from the tortured ground, ran in their thousands up the walls of the palaces of the Rich, feeding on the masonry as they went. The Rich fell screaming to the ground as their homes disappeared like marzipan. A great wind storm arose, blowing the poor people like straws into the fiery gulfs. Mountains rose up. Valleys sank. The planet sang in its misery. Even the atmosphere burned.

THE STATUE. The Son, supervising all, walked along the shore of a lava lake. There, on all the million million planets, he saw a grand statue. Smoke formed her cloak. The statue was of a woman, whose bronze hair blew in the gale. Drawing near, the Son saw that the statue moved. It was not a woman. Nor was it a statue, but something between statue and woman, and the bronze hair was of an unknown metal.

'Why do you destroy this planet?' this semi-female demanded in a deep voice.

'All planets, all million million of them, are being destroyed. The Unicrat is cancelling Galaxy Zee. The plan is not working out.'

'It is the Unicrat that is at fault. He must be destroyed.'

'The Unicrat cannot be destroyed. But you can be.'

The semi-female said in its deep and melancholy voice, 'No, I cannot be destroyed. I am the Controller of Galaxy Why, where we order things better.'

'Yes?' said the Son, with sarcasm. 'How better?'

'You, Son, have only intellect. No compassion. No emotion. So your plan can never succeed.'

'But –' exclaimed the Son in triumph – 'I can and will wipe out this planet. Together with all the million million other planets!'

THE UNION. As he spoke, the Son clapped his hands. The world began to boil. It shrank and the galaxy thereabout shrank with it, causing infernal temperatures to rise. Darkness fed on light, light snapped at the belly of the dark. A soup of matter was rapidly forming, curdling, spewing out radiation. Electrons from the outer parts of atoms were torn away, so that a stew of nuclei and electrons boiled and blazed. Total annihilation was coming within a millionth part of a second, when the semi-female clasped the Son in her mighty arms, and whisked him instantaneously away, away into Galaxy Why, to form a new union.

BANG. Space, time and energy were consumed to nothing. The entire galaxy was contained within the space of a flea's eyeball. The contraction was all but instantaneous. And then, purified, all burst forth once more in a fury of renewed energy.

The Unicrat cried in delight at such a Big Bang.

Marvells
of Utopia

They had been lovers centuries ago. Circumstances had caused them to part for different regions of the galaxy. Both served where they were most needed.

For all the invisible nanoservants in their blood, both were now becoming ready for euthanasia. But something in their love was timeless. At the peak of their passion, they had commemorated themselves in hologram. Still in that plastic cube they lived and moved as they had once been, for ever in passionate love, for ever perfect, clear of brow, and careless of the world.

It was the thousandth anniversary of the Reformed Planets' Secretary General's 'Stay your hand!' speech, as it had become known. On that occasion, the human race, severally and corporately, intellectually and emotionally, had decided to be better people and discard the bogeymen of the past. It was a fantastic operation in behavioural manipulation. And it worked.

So now the two aged lovers were called upon, from their different regions of the system, to converse together for the peepers. They met and embraced – not without the trace of tears. Millions watched.

'I admit I had forgotten you for a whole century,' she said. 'I regret it. Forgive me!'

'"A hundred years should go to praise thine eyes and on thy forehead gaze,"' he quoted, with a smile.

She gave her old creaking laugh. '"An age at least to every part, And the last age should show my heart."'

'What marvellous memories we have!'

'Marvellous indeed!'

They began to reminisce about those times when human life had taken a turn for the better, and when humanity had managed to lift itself from its birth-planet.

She wore a white bandage dress, signalling her age and comparative fragility. She opened this part of the conversation.

'It's a glorious and grand story, very surprising to those who were alive to play a part in it, all those centuries ago. I'm talking to my friend in Marsport, where he was born. Dearest, why aren't you living on a light-grav satellite at your age?'

He said, 'I'm just tidying a few matters up. I won't be here for long.' His face was clean and without whisker, his flesh taut, his eyes bright but sunken. 'So let's see what we can remember of those ancient days of early spaceflight.

'One thing is sure, our minds were less clear then – cluttered like old boxrooms . . . Our imaginations were occupied by all kinds of imaginary impossible creatures. Do you remember that strange period?'

She said, 'The human race must have been half mad. Or I suppose one should say half sane. The unfortunate generations who lived out our first thousands of years of human existence . . . well, they were still mired in dreams of a sub-human past. Nightmares, you could say.'

'Breaking away from Earth helped the process of clarification,' he said. 'The Earth was supposedly haunted by – oh, ghouls and ghosts and long-legged beasties, vampires, leprechauns, elves, gnomes, fairies, angels . . . All those fantasy creatures besetting early human life. I suppose they were born of dark forests and old houses, together with a general lack of scientific understanding.'

She said, 'You could add to that long list all the world's false gods and goddesses, the Greek gods, who gave their names to the constellations, the Baals and Isises and Roman soldier gods, the multi-armed Kali, Ganesh with the elephant's head, Allah, Jehovah with his beards and rages, dusky hags such as Astarte – oh, an endless stream of imaginary super-beings, all supposedly controlling human destiny.'

'You're right, sweetest, I forgot them.'

'The mere idea of Heaven made it a Hell on Earth . . .'

'How long ago it seems! They were all creaking floor-boards in the cellarage of the brain, inheritances from our eo-human days.'

'And what,' she said, and her voice faltered slightly, 'what will our descendants make of *us* in another million years?'

He cast his gaze downwards, showing a sign of weariness. '"Ever at my back I hear Time's winged chariot drawing near . . ."'

'"Yonder all before us lie Deserts of vast eternity". It's a consolation really, my love.' She leant forward and stroked his cheek, in an ancient gesture of affection between women and men.

Becoming the Full Butterfly

The Great Dream was a wild success, far beyond anyone's imagining. Afterwards, no one recalled exactly who had chosen Monument Valley for its staging. The organisers claimed most of the credit. No one mentioned Casper Trestle. Trestle had disappeared again.

So had much else.

Trestle was always disappearing. Three years earlier, he had been wandering in Rajasthan. In that bleak and beautiful territory, where once deer had lain down with rajahs, he came through a rainless area where the land was denuded of trees and animals; here, huts were collapsing and the people were dying of drought. Men, aged at thirty, stood motionless as scarecrows of bone, watching with sick disinterest as Casper trudged by; but Casper was accustomed to disinterest. Only termites flourished, termites and the scavenger birds wheeling overhead.

Afflicted by the parched land, Casper found his way through to a mountainous area where, miraculously, trees still grew and rivers flowed. He continued onwards, where the rugged countryside began to rise to meet the distant grandeur of the Himalayas. Plants blossomed with pendulous mauve and pink flowers like Victorian lampshades. There he met the mysterious Leigh; Leigh Tireno. Leigh was watching goats and lounging on a rock under the dappled shade of a baobab, while the bees made a low song that seemed to fill the little valley with sleep.

'Hi,' Casper said.

'Likewise,' Leigh said. He lay back on his rock, one hand stretched above his forehead shading his eyes, which were as brown as fresh honey. The nearest goat was a cloudy white like milk, and carried a little battered bell about its neck. The bell clattered in B flat as the animal rubbed its haunches against Leigh's rock.

That was all that was said. It was a hot day.

But that night, Casper dreamed a delicious dream. He found a magic guava fruit and took it into his hand. The fruit opened for him and he plunged his face into it, seeking with his tongue, sucking the seeds into his mouth, swallowing them.

Casper found a place to doss in Kameredi. Casper was lost, really a lost urchin, snub-nosed, pasty of face, with hair growing out in straggly fashion from a neglected crew-cut. Although he had never learnt manners, he maintained the docility of the defeated. And he instinctively liked Kameredi. It was a humble version of paradise. After a few days, he began to see it was orderly and sane.

Kameredi was what some of the villagers called the Place of the Law. Others denied it had or needed a name: it was simply where they lived. Their houses stood on either side of a paved street which ended as it began, in earth. Other huts stood further up the hill, their decrease in size being more than a matter of perspective. A stream ran nearby, a little gossipy flow of water which chased among boulders on its way to the valley. Watercress grew in its side pools.

The children of Kameredi were surprisingly few in number. They flew kites, wrestled with each other, caught small silver fish in the stream, tried to ride the placid goats.

The women of Kameredi washed their clothes in the stream, beating them mercilessly against rocks. The children bathed beside them, screaming with the delight of being children. Dogs roamed the area like down-and-outs, pausing to scratch or looking up at the kite-hawks which soared above the thatched roofs.

Not much work was done in Kameredi, at least as far as the men were concerned. They squatted together in their dhotis, smoking and talking, gesticulating with their slender brown arms. Where they usually met, by V.K. Bannerji's house, the ground was stained red by betel juice.

Mr Bannerji was a kind of headman of the village. Once a month, he and his two daughters walked down into the valley to trade. They went loaded with honeycombs and cheeses and returned with kerosene and sticking plaster. Casper stayed at Mr Bannerji's house, sleeping on a battered charpoy beneath the colourful clay figure of Shiva, god of destruction and personal salvation.

Casper was a dead-beat. He was now off drugs. All he wanted at present was to be left alone and sit in the sun. Every day he sat on an outcropping rock, looking down along the village street, past the lingam carved from stone, into the distance, shimmering with Indian heat. It suited him that he had found a place where men were not expected to do anything much. Boys tended goats, women fetched water.

At first, an old nervousness attended him. Wherever he walked, people smiled at him. He could not understand why.

Nor did he understand why there was no drought, no starvation in Kameredi.

He had a sort of hankering for Mr Bannerji's daughters, both of whom were beautiful. He relied on their cunctative services for food. They tittered at him behind their spread fingers, showing their white teeth. Since he could not decide which young lady he would most like to embrace upon his rope charpoy, he made no advances to either. It was easier that way.

His thoughts tended towards Leigh Tireno. When Casper got round to thinking about it, he told himself that a kind of magic hung over Kameredi. And over the bare-legged Leigh. He watched from his rock the bare-legged Leigh going about his day. Not that Leigh was much more active than anyone else; but occasionally he would climb up into the tree-clad heights above the village and disappear for several days. Or he would sit in the lotus position on his favourite boulder, holding the pose for hours at a time, eyes staring sightlessly ahead. In the evening, he would remove his dhoti and swim naked in one of the pools fed by the stream.

As it happened, Casper took it into his head to stroll along by the pool where Leigh swam.

'Hi,' he called as he passed.

'Likewise,' replied Leigh, perfecting his breast stroke. Casper could not help noticing that Leigh had a white behind, and was otherwise burnt as dark as an Indian. The daughters of Mr Bannerji moulded with their slender fingers goat's cheeses as white as Leigh's behind. It was very mysterious and a little discomfiting.

Mr Bannerji had visited the outside world. Twice in his life he had been as far as Delhi. He was the only person in Kameredi who spoke any English, apart from Casper and Leigh. Casper picked up a few words of Urdu, mainly those to do with eating and drinking. He learned from Mr Bannerji that Leigh Tireno had lived for three years in the village. He came, said Mr Bannerji, from Europe, but was of no nation. He was a magical person and must not be touched.

'You are not to be touching,' repeated Mr Bannerji, studying Casper intently with his short-sighted eyes. 'Novhere.'

The two young Bannerji ladies giggled and peeled back their skins of plantains in very slinky ways before inserting the tips into their red mouths.

A magical person. In what way could Leigh be magical? Casper asked. Mr Bannerji wobbled his head wisely, but could not or would not explain.

The people who flocked to Monument Valley, who had booked seats on the top of mesas or stood with camcorders on the roofs of coaches, had some doubts about Leigh Tireno's magical properties. It was the publicity that got to them. They had been infected by the hype from New York and California. They believed that Leigh was a messiah.

Or else they didn't care either way.

They went to Monument Valley because the notion of a sex change turned them on.

Or because the neighbours were going.

'Hell of a place to go,' they said.

When the sun went down, darkness embraced Kameredi like an old friend, with that particular mountain darkness which is a rare variant of light. The lizards go in, the geckos come out. The night-jar trills of ancient romance. The huts and houses hold in their strawy palms the dizzy golden smell of kerosene lamps. There are roti smells too, matched with the scent of boiled rice teased with strands of curried goat. The perfumes of the night are warm and chill by turns, registering on the skin like moist fingertips. The tiny world of Kameredi becomes for an hour a place of sensuality, secret from the sun. Then everyone falls asleep: to exist in another world until cock crow.

In that hidden hour, Leigh came to Casper Trestle.

Casper could hardly speak. He was half reclining on his charpoy, a hand supporting his untidy head. There stood Leigh looking down at him, with a smile as enigmatic as the most abstruse Buddha.

'Hi,' Casper said.

Leigh said, 'Likewise.'

Casper struggled into a sitting position. He clutched his toes and gazed up at his beautiful visitor, unable to produce a further word.

Without preliminary, Leigh said, 'You have been in the universe long enough to understand a little of its workings.'

Supposing this to be a question, Casper nodded his head.

'You have been in this village long enough to understand a little of its workings.' Pause. 'So I shall tell you something about it.'

This seemed to Casper very strange, despite the fact that his life had passed mainly surrounded by strange people.

'You mustn't be touched? Why not?'

When Leigh's mouth moved, it had its own kind of music, separate from the sounds it uttered. 'Because I am a dream. I may be your dream. If you touch me, you may awaken from it. Then — then where would you be?' He gave a tiny cold sound almost like a human laugh.

'Ummm,' said Casper, 'New Jersey, I guess . . .'

Whereupon Leigh continued with what he had intended to say. He said the people in Kameredi and a few villages nearby were a special sort of Rajput people. They had a special story. They had been set apart from ordinary folk by a special dream. The dream had happened four centuries ago. It was still revered, and known as the Great Law Dream.

'As a man of Kameredi respects his father,' said Leigh, 'so he respects the Great Law Dream even more.'

Four centuries ago in past time, a certain sadhu, a holy man, was dying in Kameredi. In the hours before his death, he dreamed a series of laws. These he was relating to his daughter when Death arrived, dressed in a deep shadow, to carry him away to Vishnu. Because of her purity, the holy man's daughter had special powers, and was able to bargain with Death.

The holy man's spirit left him. Death stood over them both as the woman coaxed her dead father to speak, and to continue speaking until he had related to her all the laws of his dream. Then a vapour issued from his mouth. He had cried out. His lips had become sealed with the pale seal of Death. He was buried within the hour: yet even before the prayers were chanted and the body interred, it began to decompose. So the people knew a miracle had happened in their midst.

But the laws remained for the daughter to recite.

Her head changed to the head of an elephant. In this guise of wisdom, she summoned the entire village before her. All abased themselves and fasted for seven days while she recited to them the laws of the Great Law Dream.

The people had followed the laws of the Great Law Dream ever since.

The laws guided their conduct. The laws concerned worldly things, not spiritual, for, if the worldly matters were properly observed, then the spiritual would follow.

The laws taught the people how to live contentedly within their families and peacefully with each other. The laws taught them to be kind to strangers. The laws taught them to despise worldly goods of which they had no need. The laws taught them how to survive.

Those survival laws had, of all the laws, been most rigorously followed for four centuries, ever since the sadhu was taken by Death. For instance, the laws spoke of breath and water. Breath, the spirit of human life, water the spirit of all life. They taught how to conserve water, and how a little should be set aside for human use every day, so much spared for the animals, so much for plants and trees. The laws taught how to cook with the best conservation of fuel and rice, and how to eat healthily, and how to drink moderately and enjoyably.

Speaking of moderation, the laws declared that happiness often lay in the silence of human tongues. Happiness was important to health. Health was most important to women, who had charge of the family cooking pot.

The laws spoke of the dangers of women bearing too

many children, and of too many mouths to be fed in consequence. They told of certain pebbles to be found in the bed of the river, which the women could insert into their yonis to prevent fertilisation. The smoothness of the stones, brought down from the snows of the Himalayas, and their dimensions, were minutely described.

Nakedness was no crime; before the gods, all humans went naked.

Behaviour too was described. Two virtues, said the laws, made for human happiness, and should be inculcated even into small children: self-abnegation and forgiveness.

'Love those near you and those distant,' said the laws. 'Then you will be able to love yourself. Love the gods. Never pretend to them, or you will deceive yourself.'

So much for the spiritual part. Instructions on the way to bake chapatis took up more time.

Finally, the Great Law Dream was clear about the trees. Trees must be conserved. Goats must not eat of trees or saplings, or be permitted to eat the smallest seedling. No tree less than a hundred years old must be cut down for fuel or building material. Only the tops of trees, when they grew over six feet high, might be used for this: in that way, Kameredi and surrounding villages would have shade and a good climate. Birds and beasts would survive which would otherwise perish. The countryside would not be denuded and become a desert.

If the people looked to these laws of nature, then nature would look to them.

So spoke the sadhu in his hour of departure from this world. So said the head of the elephant, echoing him.

As Leigh Tireno spoke concerning these matters, he seemed to become, as he claimed he was, a dream. His eyes became large, his eyelashes like the tips of thorn bushes, his simple face grave, his lips a musical instrument through which issued musics of wisdom.

He said that ever since the holy man's daughter gave forth the Great Law Dream through her blue elephant's head, the people of Kameredi had followed those precepts scrupulously. Nearby villages, having heard the laws, had not bothered with them. They had denuded their woods, eaten too greedily, begotten many children with greedy mouths. So the people of Kameredi lived happily, while less disciplined people perished, and passed away, and were forgotten on the stream of time.

'What about sex?' Casper asked.

And Leigh answered calmly, 'Sex and reproduction are Shiva's gift. They are our fortification against decay. Like Shiva, they can also destroy.' He gave Casper a smile of sorrowful beauty and left the Bannerji house, walking out lightly into the dark. The night-jar sang to him as he went his way. The night itself nestled on his slender shoulder.

'You want to promote an event where two crazy people sleep together?' The question was asked incredulously in a publicity office in New York. Fifth Avenue in the high thirties. Sale time again in Macy's.

'Are we talking hetero, gay, lesbian or what here?'

'Have they figgered out a new way of doing it? A short cut or something?'

'Forget it, you can see people screwing back home every night, in the safety of your own apartment.'

'They don't only screw, these two. They plan to have a very basic dream.'

'Dream, did you say? You want us to rent Monument

Valley for some fucking queers to have a dream? Get the fuck out of here!'

Leigh was climbing naked from the pool. Little rivulets of water ran from the watershed of his back down the length of his long legs. His pubic hair twinkled like a spider's web loaded with morning dew. Casper could hardly bear to look. He trembled, unable to make out what was wrong with him. When did he ever experience such desire?

Looking in the grass to check no leeches were about, Leigh folded himself on a rock. He squeezed water from his hair with one hand. Sighing with contentment, he closed his eyes. He turned his faultless face up to the Sun, as though to return its rays.

'Really, you are a mess, Casper. This place should help you to get better, to mend – to be at peace inwardly with yourself.'

It was the first time he had spoken in this fashion.

'Those dream laws,' Casper said, to change the subject. 'They're a lot of Indian hokum really, yep?'

'We all have a sense at the back of our minds that there was once a golden, primal time, when all was well with us – maybe in infancy.'

'Not me.'

'The Great Law Dream represents such a time for a whole community. You and I, my sad Casper, come from a culture where all – almost all – has been lost. Consumption instead of communication. Commercialism instead of contentment. Isn't that so?'

Standing on the spot, looking sulky and secretly contemplating Leigh's exposed body, Casper said, 'I never had nothing to consume.'

'But you want it. You're all grab at heart, Casper!' He sat up suddenly, lids still shielding his honeyed eyes. 'Don't you remember back home, how they ate, how everyone ate and yet hardly breathed? The breath of life! How there was this sentimental cult of childhood, yet all the while kids were neglected, beaten, taught only negatives?'

Casper nodded. 'I sure remember that.' He fingered the scar on his shoulder.

'People don't know themselves back there, Casper. They cannot take a deep breath and know themselves. Knowledge they have – facts. Wisdom, not so. Most are hung up on sex. Women are trapped in male bodies, thousands of gay men long to be hetero . . . Humanity has fallen into a bad dream, rejecting spirituality, clinging to self – to lowly biological origins.'

He opened his eyes then, to scrutinise Casper. In the branches of the banyan nearby, pigeons cooed as if in mockery.

'I'm not so freaked out as I was.' Casper found nothing else to say.

'I came here to develop what was in me . . . If you travel far enough, you discover what you originally were.'

'That's true. Like I've put on a bit of weight.'

Leigh appeared to ignore the remark. 'As our breathing is automatic, so there are archetypes, I've come to believe, which guide our behaviour, if we allow them. A kind of automatic response.'

'This is over my head, Leigh. Sorry. Talk sense, will you?'

The gentle smile. 'You do understand. You do understand, and reject what is unfamiliar. Try thinking of archetypes as master – and mistress – figures, such as you encounter in fairy tales, *The Beauty and the Beast*, for instance. Guiding our behaviour like very basic programming in a computer.'

'Grow up, Leigh! Fairy tales!'

'Archetypes have been set at nothing in our Western culture. So they're at war with our superficiality. We need them. Archetypes reach upwards to the rarefied heights of great music. And down into the soil of our being, down to the obscure realms beyond language, where only our dreaming selves can reach them.'

Casper scratched his crotch. He was embarrassed at being talked to as if he was an intelligent man. It had happened so rarely.

'I've never heard of archetypes.'

'But you meet them in your sleep — those personages who are you, yet not you. The strangers you are familiar with.'

He scratched his chin instead of his crotch. 'You think dreams are that important?'

Leigh's was a gentle laugh, not as mocking as the doves'. 'This village is proof of it. If only . . . if only there were some way you and I could dream a Great Law Dream together. For the benefit of all humanity.'

'Sleep together, you mean? Hey! You won't allow that! You're tabu.'

'Perhaps only to a carnal touch . . .' He slid down and confronted Casper face to face. 'Casper, try! Save yourself. Release yourself. Let everything be changed. It's not impossible. It's easier than you think. Don't cling to the chrysalis state — be the full butterfly!'

Casper Trestle took dried meat and fruit and climbed up into the mountains above Kameredi. There he remained and thought and experienced what some would call visions.

Some days, he fasted. Then it seemed to him that someone walked beside him in the forest. Someone wiser than he. Someone he knew intimately yet was unable to recognise. His thoughts that were not thoughts streamed from him like water.

He saw himself in a still pool. His hair grew to his shoulders and he went barefoot.

This is what he said to himself, scooping together fragments of reflection in the cloth of his mind:

'He's so beautiful. He must be Truth itself. Me, I'm a sham. I've cocked up my entire life. I've had it cocked up for me. No, at last I must grab a slice of the blame. That way, I take control. I won't enjoy being a victim. Not no more. I'm going to change. I too can be beautiful, someone else's dream . . .

'I've been in the wrong dream. The stupid indulgent dream of time. The abject dream of wealth beyond dreams. Spiritual destitution.

'Something's happened to me. From today, from now, I will be different.

'Okay, I'm going crackers, but I will be different. I will change. Already I'm changing. I'm becoming the full butterfly.'

After a few nights, when the new moon rose, he went to look at his reflection again.

For the first time he saw – though in tatters – beauty. He wrapped his arms around himself. In the pool, from tiny throats, frogs cried out that there was no night.

He danced by the pool. 'Change, you froggies!' he called. 'If I can do it, anyone can do it.' They had done it.

Somewhere distantly, when the Moon sank into the welcoming maw of the mountains, he heard dismal roaring, as if creatures fought to the death in desolate swamps.

From the hoarse throats of machines, diesel fumes spewed. Genman Timber PLC was getting into action for another day. Guys in hard hats and jeans issued from the canteen. They tossed their cigarette butts into the mud, heading for their tractors and chainsaws. The previous day they had cleared four square kilometres of forest in the mountain some distance above Kameredi.

The Genman camp was a half formed circle of portable cabins. Generators roared, pumping electricity and air-conditioning round the site. Immense mobile cranes, brought to this remote area at great expense, loaded felled trees on to a string of lorries.

There were many more trees to go. The trees stood silent, awaiting the bite of metal teeth. In times to come, far from the Himalayas, they would form elements in furniture sold from showrooms in wasteland outside Rouen or Atlanta or Munich or Madrid. Or they would become crates containing oranges from Tel-Aviv, grapes from Cape Province, tea from Guangzhou. They would form scaffolding on high-rises in Osaka, Beijing, Budapest, Manila. Or fake tourist figurines sold in Bali, Berlin, London, Aberdeen, Buenos Aires.

It was early yet at the Genman site. The sun came grumbling up into layers of mist. Loudspeakers played rock music over the area. Overseers were cursing. Men were tense as they gunned their engines into life, or joked to postpone the moments when they had to exert themselves in the forests.

Bloated fuel carriers started up. Genman bulldozers turned like animals in pain on their caterpillar tracks, to throw up muck as they headed for their designated tasks.

The whole camp was a sea of mud.

Soon the trees would come crashing down, exposing ancient lateritic soils. And someone would be making a profit, back in Calcutta, California, Japan, Honolulu, Adelaide, England, Bermuda, Bombay, Zimbabwe, you name it . . .

Action started. Then the rain began, blowing ahead in full sail from the south-west.

'Shit,' said the men, but carried on. They had their bonuses to think of.

The new Casper slept. And had a terrible dream. It was like no other dream. As life is like a dream, this dream was like life.

His brain burned with it. He rose before dawn and stumbled through the aisles of the forest. His path lay downward. For two days and nights he travelled without food. He saw many old palaces sinking down into the mud, like great illuminated liners into an arctic sea. He saw things running and gigantic lizards giving birth. Eyes of amber, eyes of azure, breasts of bronze, adorned his track. So he returned to Kameredi and found it all despoiled.

What had been a harmonious village, with people and animals living together – he knew now how rare and precious this was – was no more. All had gone. Men and women, animals, hens, buildings, the little stream – all gone.

It was as if Kameredi had never been.

The rains had not fallen on Kameredi. The rains had fallen at higher altitudes. With the forests felled, upper streams had overflowed. Tides of mud flowed downhill. Before that chilly lava flow, everything gave way.

The people of Kameredi had been unprepared. The Great Law Dream had said nothing of this inundation. They were carried away, breathing dirt, drowned, submerged, finished.

And Casper saw himself walking over the desecrated ground, looking at the bodies growing like uncouth tubers from the sticky mess. He saw himself fall in a swoon to the ground.

In Monument Valley, gigantic stadia were being constructed at top speed. Bookings were being taken for seats as yet not fabricated. Emergency roads were being built. Notices, signs, public restrooms, were going up. Washington was becoming concerned. All kinds of large-scale scams were being set in motion. The League of Indigenous American Peoples was holding protest meetings.

A well-known Italian artist was wrapping up one of the mesas in pale blue plastic.

When Casper awoke, all knowledge seemed to have left him. He looked about. The room was dark. Everything was obscure except for Leigh Tireno. Leigh stood by the charpoy, seeming to glow.

'Hi,' Casper whispered.

'Likewise,' said Leigh. They gazed upon each other as if upon summer landscapes choked with corn.

'Er, how about sex?' Casper asked.

'Our fortification against decay.'

Casper lay back, wondering what had happened. As if reading his thoughts, Leigh said, 'We knew you were in the mountains. I knew you were having a strong and terrible dream. I came with four women. They carried you back here. You are safe.'

'Safe!' Casper screamed. Suddenly his mind was clear. He staggered from the bed and made for the door. He was in Mr Bannerji's house and it was not destroyed, and Mr Bannerji's daughters lived.

Outside, the sun reigned over its peaceful village. Hens strutted between buildings. Children played with a puppy, men spat betel juice, women stood statuesque by the dhobi place.

Mud did not exist.

No corpses tried to swim down a choked street.

'Leigh, I had a dream as real as life itself. As life is a dream, so my dream was life. I must tell Mr Bannerji. It is a warning. Everyone must take their livestock and move to a safer place to live. But will they believe me?'

A month passed away for ever before they found a new place. It was three days' journey from the old place, facing south from the top of a fertile valley. The women complained at its steepness. But here it would be safe. There was water and shade. Trees grew. Mr Bannerji and others went into a town and traded livestock for cement. They rebuilt Kameredi in the new place. The women complained at the depth of the new watercourse. Goats ate the cement and got sick.

An ancient hag with a diamond at her nostril recited the Great Law Dream for all to hear, one evening when the stars resembled more diamonds and a moon above the new Kameredi swelled and became pregnant with light. Slowly the new place became their familiar Kameredi. Small boys with a dog sent to inspect the old place returned and reported it destroyed by a great mud flow, as if the earth had regurgitated itself.

Casper was embraced by all. He had dreamed truthfully. The villagers celebrated their escape from death. The village enjoyed twenty-four hours of drinking and rejoicing, during which time Casper lay with both of the Bannerji ladies, his limbs entwined with theirs, his warmth mingled with theirs, his juices with theirs.

In their yonis the ladies had placed smooth stones, as decreed in the laws. Casper kept the stones afterwards, as souvenirs, as trophies, as sacred memorials of blessed events.

Leigh Tireno disappeared. Nobody knew his whereabouts. He was gone so long that even Casper found he could live without him.

After another moon had waxed and waned, Leigh returned. His hair had grown long, and was tied by ribbon over one shoulder. He had decorated his face. His lips were reddened. He wore a sari. Under the sari, breasts swelled.

'Hi,' Leigh said.

'Likewise,' said Casper, holding out his arms. 'Life in New Kameredi is made new. All's changed. I've changed. It's the full butterfly. And you look more beautiful than ever.'

'I've changed. I am a woman. That is the discovery I had to make. I merely dreamed I was a man. It was the wrong dream for me, and I have at last awakened from it.'

To Casper's surprise, he was not as surprised as he might have been. He was becoming accustomed to the miraculous life.

'You have a yoni?'

Leigh lifted his – her – sari and demonstrated. She had a yoni, ripe as guavas.

'It's beautiful. How about sex now?'

'It's fortification against decay. Shiva's gift. It can also destroy.' She smiled. Her voice was softer than before. 'As I have told you. Be patient.'

'What became of your lingam? Did it drop off?'

'It crawled away into the undergrowth. In the forest, I menstruated for the first time. The moon was full. Where the blood fell, there a guava tree grew.'

'If I found the tree and ate of its fruit . . .'

He tried to touch her but she backed away. 'Casper, forget your little private business for a while. If you have really changed, you can look beyond your personal horizons to something wider, grander.'

Casper felt ashamed. He dropped his gaze to the floor, where ants crawled, as they had done even before the gods awoke and painted their faces blue.

'I'm sorry. Instruct me. Be my sadhu.'

She arranged herself among the ants in the lotus position. 'The logging in the hills. It is based more on greed than necessity. It needs to stop. Not just the logging, but all it stands for in the mercenary world. Contempt for the dignity of nature.'

It sounded like a tall order to Casper. But when he complained, Leigh coolly said that logging was very minor and nature was vast. 'We must dream together.'

'How do you manage that?'

'A powerful dream, in order to change more than little Kameredi, more than ourselves. A healing dream, together. As we have dreamed separately and succeeded. As all men and women dream separately – always separately. But we will dream together.'

'Touching?'

She smiled. 'You still must change. Change is a continuity.

There are no comfort stations on the road to perfection.'

Within his breast, his heart jumped for fear and hope at the wonderful words. 'The things you understand . . . I worship you.'

'One day, I may worship you.'

Special units of the National Guard had been drafted in to control the crowds. Half of Utah and Arizona was cordoned off by razor wire. Counter-insurgency posts had been established; Washington was wary of dream-makers. Tanks, trucks, armed personnel carriers, patrolled everywhere. Special elevated ways had been erected. Armed police bikers roared along them, licensed to fire down on the crowds if trouble was brewing. Heligunships circled overhead, cracking the eardrums of Monument Valley with spiteful noise.

They supervised a sprawling site bearing the hallmarks of an interior landscape of manic depression.

Someone said, 'Seems like they are shooting the war movie to end all war movies.'

Private automobiles had been banned. They were corralled in huge parks as far north as Blanding, Utah; at Shiprock, New Mexico, in the east; and at Tuba City, Arizona, to the south. The Hopis and Navajos were making a killing. A slew of cafés, bars and restaurants had sprung up from nowhere. Along authorised routes, lurid entertainments of various kinds sprang forth like paintboxes bursting. Many carried giant effigies of Leigh Tireno, looking at her best, above booths with such come-ons as 'Change Your Sex By Hypnosis – PAINLESS!' No one mentioned Casper Trestle.

How the good folk jostled on their way to the spectacle! It was mighty hot there, in the crowded desolation; sweat rose like a mist, an illness above the heaving shoulders.

Bacteria were having a great time. Countless city people, unaccustomed to walking more than a block, found the quarter mile from a Park and Ride bus drop more than they could take, and collapsed into the many field ambulance units. Rest was charged at $25 an hour. Some walked on singing or sobbing, according to taste. Pickpockets moved among the crowd, elbowing hot-gospellers of many kinds. The preachers preached their tunes of damnation. It was not difficult for the unprivileged, as blisters formed on their heels, to believe that the end of the world was nigh – or at least heaving into sight from the seas of misery, a kind of 'Jaws' from the nether regions – or that the whole universe might sizzle down into a little white dot, like when you turned off the TV at two in the sullen Bronx morning. Could be, ending was best. Maybe with this possibility in mind, a fair percentage of the adults stomped along like cattle, pressing fast food to their mouths or slurping sweet liquids. A fat woman, hemmed in by heated bodies, was hit simultaneously by congestion and digestion; her cries as she cartwheeled among the marching legs were drowned by sporadic ghetto music from a multitude of receivers. Every orifice was stuffed. It was the law. At least no one was smoking. Varieties of bobbing caps amid the throng indicated children, big and little hobbledehoys fighting to get through first, yelling, screaming, gobbling popcorn as they went. Underfoot, all kinds of coloured cartons and wrappers of non-biodegradable material were trampled in the dust, along with the tumbling bodies, the gobs of pink gum, the discarded items of clothing, the ejected tampons, the lost soles. It was a real media event, as much a crowd-puller as the World Series.

*

Casper had set the whole vast scheme in motion. Now he was responsible only for himself and Leigh. Human nature was beyond his control. He stood in the middle of a mile-wide arena where John Wayne had once ridden hell-for-leather. Mr V.K. Bannerji was with him, terrified by the sheer blast of public attention.

'Vill it vork?' he asked Casper. 'Otherwise ve shall have wiolence.'

But at six in the evening, when the shadows of the giant mesas grew like long, blunt, black teeth over the land, a bell rang and silence fell. A slight breeze arose, mitigating the heat, cooling many a feverish armpit. The pale blue plastic in which one of the mesas had been wrapped, crackled slightly. Otherwise all was at last still – still as it had been in the millennia before the human race existed.

A king-size bed stood raised in the middle of the arena. Leigh waited by the side of the bed. She removed her clothes without coquetry, turning about once in a full circle, so that all could see she was now a woman. She climbed into the bed.

Casper removed his clothes, also turned about to demonstrate that he was a man, and climbed in beside Leigh. He touched her.

They put their arms about each other and fell asleep.

Gently, music arose from the assembled Boston Pops Orchestra. Tchaikovsky's waltz from 'The Sleeping Beauty'. The organisers felt this composition was particularly appropriate on this occasion. In the million-strong audience women wept, kids threw up as quietly as possible. Before their television screens all round the world, people were weeping and throwing up into plastic bowls.

It was an ancient dream they dreamed, welling from the brain's ancient core. The beings that paraded across a primal tapestry of fields wore stiff antique garb. In these personages was vested an untroubled power over human behaviour. An untroubled archetypal power.

Before sex was life, aspiring upwards like spring water. After the advent of sexual reproduction came consciousness. Before consciousness dawned, dreams prevailed. Such dreams form the language of the archetypes.

In the espousal of a technological civilisation, those ancient personages had been neglected, despised. Hero, warrior, matron, maiden true, wizard, mother, wise-man too – finally their paths were bent to sow in human lives dissent. In disarray a billion lives were spent: war, rapine, mental torment, dismay . . . But LeighCas in the tongue of dream vowed to these forces to redeem the time, asked in return – it seems – that male and female might be free of crime . . . to live in better dreams . . .

Casper struggled up through layers of blanketing sleep. He lay unsure of himself, or where he was. Much had transpired, that he knew: a shift in consciousness. The dark head of the woman Leigh lay on his breast. Opening his eyes, he saw that above him flared an Impressionist sky, encompassing cinnamon and maroon banners of sunset waving at feverish rate from horizon to far horizon.

Prompted by deep instinct, he felt down between his legs. He dug into a furry nest and found lips there. What they told him wordlessly was strange and new. He wondered for a while if, soggy from the miracle sleep, he was feeling her by mistake. Gently, he stirred her away from his breast . . . his breasts . . . *her* breasts.

When Leigh opened her eyes and looked honey-coloured at Casper, her gaze was remote. Slowly her lips curved into a smile.

'Likewise,' she remarked, slipping a finger into Casper's yoni. 'How about a fortification against decay?'

The multitudes were leaving the auditorium. The aircraft were heading like eagles back to their nests. The tanks were pulling out. The Italian artist was unwrapping his mesa. Imagining he heard tree-cutting machines falling silent in distant forests, Mr Bannerji sat on the side of the bed, to cover his short-sighted eyes and weep with joy – the joy that survives in the midst of sorrow.

Immersed in their thoughts, the short-sighted multitudes went away. The different dream was taking effect. No one jostled. Something in their unity of posture, the bent shoulders, the bowed heads, was reminiscent of figures in an ancient frieze.

Here or there, a cheek, an eyeball, a bald head, reflected back the imperial colours of the sky, arbitrary yellows denoting happiness or pain, red meaning fire or passion, the blues of nullity or reflection. Nothing remained but land and sky – for ever at odds, for ever a unity. The mesas were standing up into the velvet, ancient citadels built without hands to commemorate distant time.

Although the multitude was silent as it departed, its multiple jaws not moving, a kind of murmur rose from its ranks.

The still, sad music of humanity.

The day's death flew its colours, increasingly sombre. It was sunset: the dawn of a new age.

A WHITER MARS

A SOCRATIC DIALOGUE OF
TIMES TO COME

SHE We want to present a history of the development of
Mars, and how we have progressed spiritually. It is a
glorious and surprising story, a history of human
society understanding and recreating itself. While I
am speaking to you from Mars, my Earthbound avatar
is speaking to you from our old parent planet. Let us
cast our minds back before everything changed, to
the Age of Estrangement, when nobody had ever set
foot on Earth's neighbouring planet.

HE So. Back to the twenty-first century and a barren
planet. The first arrivals on Mars found an empty
world, free of all the imaginary creatures which have
been supposed to haunt the Earth: the ghosts and
ghouls and long-legged beasties, the vampires, the
leprechauns, the elves and fairies – all those fantasy
creatures which beset human life, born of dark
forests, old houses, and ancient brains.

SHE   You've forgotten the gods and goddesses, the Greek gods who gave their names to the constellations, the Baals and Isises and Roman soldier gods, the vengeful Almighty of the Old Testament, Allah — all imaginary super-beings which supposedly controlled mankind's behaviour before humanity could control itself.

HE   You're right, I forgot them. They were all creaking floorboards in the cellars of the brain, inheritances from eo-human days. Earth was over-populated with both real and imaginary persons. Mars was blessedly free of all that. On Mars, you could start anew. It's true the men and women who arrived on Mars had a lot of conflicting Mars legends in their heads . . .

SHE   Oh, you mean that old stuff. Percival Lowell's Mars of the canals and the dying culture. I still have a kind of nostalgia for that grand sunset vision — wrong in reality, right as imagery. And Edgar Rice Burroughs's *Barsoom* . . .

HE   And all the horrors which earlier humanity invented to populate Mars — H.G. Wells's invaders of Earth, rather than the gentle Hrossa and pfifltriggi of C.S. Lewis's *Malacandra*.

SHE   Life, you see, always this bizarre preoccupation with life, however fantastic. Tokens of the insufficiency of our own lives.

HE   But the first men who went to Mars came from a technological age. They harboured another idea in their heads. Certainly they were hoping to find life of some sort, archebacteria being reckoned most likely. They nourished the idea of terraforming the Red Planet and turning it into a sort of inferior second Earth.

SHE   Having at last managed to reach another planet, they desired to make it like Earth! The idea seems strange to us now.

HE   They had not acquired the habit of living away from Earth. 'Terraforming' was an engineer's dream – a novelty. Their perceptions had to change. They stood there, gaping – aware for the first time of the magnitude of the task and of its aggressive nature. Every planet has its own sanctity.

SHE   Even at the most impressive moments in life, a voice seems to speak within us, the mind communing with itself. Percy Bysshe Shelley was the first to recognise this duality. In a poem on Mont Blanc, he speaks of standing watching a waterfall and says:

> *Dizzy Ravine! – and when I gaze on thee*
> *I seem as in a trance sublime and strange*
> *To muse on my own separate phantasy,*
> *My own, my human mind, which passively*
> *Now renders and receives fast influencings,*
> *Holding an unremitting interchange*
> *With the clear universe of things around . . .*

HE   Yes, the words strike to the very essence of human perceptions. As phenomenology declares, our inner discourse shapes our outward perception. I'll remind you that the great Martian expedition was not the first scientific excursion which set out to discover a new world. It too had trouble with its perceptions.

SHE   You're speaking of the way the West was won in the case of North America? The slaughter of the Indian nations, the killing of buffalo? Wasn't all that a primitive kind of terraforming?

HE   I was referring to the expedition of Captain James
Cook in H.M.S. *Endeavour* to the South Seas. In his
three hundred and sixty-six ton wooden ship Cook
eventually circumnavigated the globe. The
Endeavour was commissioned to observe the 1769
transit of Venus across the face of the Sun, among
other objectives. The choice of Joseph Banks, then
only twenty-three, as scientific observer was a good
one. Banks had a trained connoisseur's eye.

It was regarded by the enlightened Royal Society
as vital that accurate drawings should accompany
written descriptions of all new discoveries. Banks's
artists had their problems. Scientific diagrams of
landscapes and plants and animals were made, but
artistry also crept in. Drawing faithful records of the
native peoples of the Pacific was beggared by the preconceptions of the time. Alexander Buchan took an
ethnographic view, drawing groups of natives free
from the conventions of neo-classical style; whereas
Sydney Parkinson disposed of them according to the
dictates of composition. In Johann Zoffany's famous
canvas, *The Death of Cook*, many of the participants
in that picture assume classical postures, presumably to increase the air of Greek tragedy.

Thus the unfamiliar was made palatable for the
folks back home, was made to bend to their preconceptions.

SHE   Mmm. I see what you're getting at. Behind the difficulties of coming to terms with the unknown lay a
philosophical problem, typical of that century. Were
the misfortunes attendant on mankind owed to a
departure from, a defiance of, natural law – or was it
that mankind could raise itself above the brute beasts

only by improving on and distancing himself from nature? The city-dweller or the Noble Savage?

HE   Exactly. The discovery of the Society Islands favoured the former idea, that of New Zealand and Australia the latter.

Australia and New Zealand, when their barren shores were first sighted, fostered the concept of improvement and progress. When Captain Arthur Phillip founded the first penal colony in Australia, at Port Jackson in 1788, he rejoiced in an eighteenth-century version of terraforming. Down went the trees, away went the wild life – including the natives – the area was flattened, and Phillip declared, 'By degrees large spaces are opened, plans are formed, lines marked, and a prospect at least of future regularity is clearly discerned, and is made the more striking by the recollection of former confusion.' Ah, the straight line! – the marker of civilisation, of capitalism!

The overwhelming belief in *conquering nature* – in somehow distancing ourselves from nature, from something of which we are an inescapable part – prevailed for at least two centuries.

SHE Possibly this dichotomy of perception was reinforced by Cartesian dualism, which made a sharp distinction between mind and body – the sort of thing Shelley spoke against. A metaphorical beheading . . .

HE   I'm unsure about that. It may be as you say.

SHE What we need to bear in mind is that a belief can take rather firm hold once it circulates among the population. No matter if it's totally erroneous. Even in these days of interplanetary travel, half the population of Earth still believes that the Sun orbits the Earth, rather than vice versa. What conclusions do you draw from that – other than that ignorance has more gravitational weight than wisdom?

HE   Or that we are more hive-minded than we care to believe?

SHE   Well, let's get back to Mars and those first arrivals here.

HE   Try to recall what the situation was in those days. With the growth in economic power of the Pacrim countries in the twenty-first century, the International Dateline had been removed to the centre of the Atlantic, and American trade was locked into that of its Asian neighbours. The cost of all Martian expeditions was met by a consortium, formed by US, Pacrim and EU space agencies. That was EUPACUS, a long-forgotten acronym. However, the UN, then under a powerful and far-sighted General Secretary, George Bligh, brought Mars under its own jurisdiction. Once you were on Mars, you came under Martian law, not under the laws of your own country.

SHE   It was a sensible provision. A lesson had been learnt from the days when Antarctica had been a continent set aside for science. Just occasionally we manage to learn from history! We wanted the Red Planet to be a White Mars – a planet set aside for science.

HE   That's an ancient battlecry!

SHE   Old battlecries still retain their power. In the mid-twenty-first century, there was a movement on Earth called APIUM – the Association for the Protection and Integrity of an Unspoilt Mars. It was regarded as a rag-taggle of eccentrics and Greens at first. APIUM wanted to preserve Mars as it had been for millions of years, as a kind of memorial to early man's early dreams. Their claim was that every environment has its sanctity, and sufficient environments had been ruined on Earth without starting out at once to monkey with another planet – an entire planet.

However, the people who landed on Mars in that first expedition had to justify costs. They were going to prepare to terraform it. It was a foregone conclusion for them. They were bound by the pressures of their rather primitive societies.

HE   Ah, yes, *terraforming*! That word and concept coined by a SF writer, by name Jack Williamson. How alluring and advanced it was when first coined. It was another of those ideas which took root easily in the fertile soil of the human mind.

SHE   Yes. There was nothing sinister about it. The astronauts simply took the idea for granted. It was a part of their mythology – meaning an old way of thought. They imagined they'd improve the planet and make it like Earth. They had glowing computer designs to seduce them, showing all of Mars looking like the Cotswolds on a sunny day.

HE   But they also carried in their minds opposed preconceptions. Mars as a rubbish dump of rock, 'suitable for development', like something from a diagram of 'Nuclear Winter' – that old guilt-myth – or Mars as a heavenly body, formidable, aloof, enduring. Similar to the two opposed ideas that Captain Cook had held three centuries earlier. And—

SHE   They left their ships and stood there, like stout Cortez, silent upon a peak in Darien in Keats's poem, with the whole vista of the planet confronting them, and—

HE   And?

SHE   And they knew – it was that discourse of Shelley's between the outer and inner world – they *knew* that terraforming was just a dream, a terrestrial city-dweller's computer phobia. It was undesirable. To use an old term, it was blasphemous, against nature. You know how city-dwellers fear nature. In a kind of vision, they saw that this environment must not be destroyed. That it carried a message, an austere message: *Rethink! You have achieved much – achieve more! Rethink!*

HE   Rethink – and re-feel – because it was experience which brought a revolution in their understanding. They knew as they stood there they were at a turning point in history. Yet, you see, some people claim this vital decision not to terraform sprang from a powerful speech by UN Secretary George Bligh, who argued against it. His words were often quoted: 'Terraforming is a clever idea which may or may not work. But cleverness is a lesser thing than reverence. We must have reverence for Mars as it has always existed. We cannot destroy the millions of years of its solitude merely for cleverness. Stay your hand!'

SHE   You believe those words of Bligh's were in the astronauts' minds when they landed?

HE   I partly believe so. I *wish* to believe so because staying the hand is often a better, if a less popular, way to proceed than conquest. Anyhow, they did stay their hands. It proved the beginning of a tide in the affairs of men. Fortunately, you couldn't exploit Mars: there were no natural resources to exploit – no oil or fossil fuels, because there had never been forests. Limited underground reservoirs of water. Just – just that amazing empty world, so long the target of mankind's dreams and speculations, a desert rolling ever onward through space.

SHE The old-fashioned word 'space', had by then been relegated to the etymological museum, by the way. That highway of teeming particles was now known as 'matrix'.

HE Okay. Thousands on thousands of young folk desired to visit Mars, just as, two centuries earlier, they had walked, rolled or ridden westwards across the face of North America. The UN had to formulate rules for visitors. Two categories of people were permitted to go, travelling uncomfortably in EUPACUS ships: the YEAs and the DOPs. (*Laughs*)

SHE It was a sensible arrangement. Or at least it worked, given the difficulties of the journey. The YEAs were Young Educated Adults. They had to pass an examination to qualify. The DOPs were Distinguished Older Persons. They were selected by their communities. The cost of an Earth-Mars round trip was high. DOPs were paid for by their communities. The YEAs paid in work, doing a year's community service before their journey.

HE So the giant fish farms off Galapagos and Scapa Flow, and the bird ranches of the Canadian north, and the vineyards of the Gobi were developed . . . all by voluntary labour.

SHE And the afforestation of most of the Outback in Australia.

HE And of the great flow of people who went to Mars, that wonderful new Ayers Rock in the sky, to meditate, to explore, to honeymoon, to realize themselves – all found themselves up against the reality of the cosmos. All stood there in awe, breathing in the laws of the universe.

SHE And one of them said, marvelling, 'And that I have come here to experience all this means I am the most extraordinary thing in the entire galaxy.'

HE Then came the crash!

SHE Oh yes, just when minds were changing everywhere! And the crash marked the end of a certain exploitive chain of thought. Pundits in 2085 called it the end of the Twentieth Century Nightmare. The consortium EUPACUS collapsed. It was a case of internal corruption. Billions of dollars had been embezzled and, when the figures were examined, the whole company fell apart.

EUPACUS had a monopoly on interplanetary travel, and on all travel arrangements. All that traffic stopped. Five thousand visitors were on Mars at the time, together with two thousand administrators, technicians and scientists – Mars of course makes an excellent observatory for studying Jupiter and its moons.

Seven thousand people – all stranded here!

HE But Mars is a big desert island. By this time, it was a complex community, lacking Wild West atmosphere, with serious business to do. There were no guns on Mars; no mind-destroying drugs; there was no currency, only limited credit.

SHE Another important thing. No animals. For there was no grazing or fodder to be had, no animals lived on Mars, except for a few cats. Vegetarianism became a positive thing rather than a negative. The habit was emulated by terrestrials. In fact, renewed concern for animals by demonstrations and lobbying, induced many governments to bring in Animal Rights laws. A revulsion to rearing animals for slaughter and human consumption was widespread. The human conscience was getting up off the couch!

HE   You must be mistaken about the animals. I remember seeing documentaries showing your Martian domes full of bright birds. And there were fish, too.

SHE   Oh, birds and fish, yes, but no animals. The birds were genetically manipulated macaws and parrots. Instead of squawking, they sang sweetly. They were allowed to fly free in limited areas of the main domes, the 'tourist' domes. They were prized. No one attempted to kill and eat them during the period when Mars was isolated.

HE   So the Martians remained cut off, luckily under wise leaders. During the period of isolation, water – the fossil water from underground reservoirs – was strictly rationed. It was needed for agriculture and went through electrolysis to provide necessary oxygen. The isolated community had reason to cohere. Without coherence there was no chance of survival.

SHE   The multi-billion collapse of EUPACUS brought financial crisis to the business centres of Earth, to LA, Seoul, Beijing, London, Paris, Frankfurt. The disillusion with *laissez-faire* capitalism was complete. So much so that 'Stay your hand!' became a popular phrase. Stay your hand from grasping another icecream, another beer, another car, another house! You stayed your hand out of pride.

It was five years before a limited flight schedule with Mars was re-established. By then the idea of community service had sunk in, reinforcing the concept of the world's population as a unit, and as part of Earth's necessary biota. Discovering that the Mars community had achieved a frugal utopia, that all there were lean but fit, was a cause for great rejoicing – most nationalities had one or more representative members on White Mars.

HE   The Martian example hastened the swing away from exploitive capitalism towards the managerialism that had already begun. *Laissez-faire* passed away in its sleep, as communism had done before it. The epoch of peaceful Earth opened, with leadership concentrating on integrating its component parts, and a general tendency to behave more like park-keepers than robber barons.

SHE Ah, but with the increase in YEA and DOP pilgrims to the heroic White Mars, the planet ran out of water. The underground reservoirs, such as they were, had been drained dry. It looked like the end of a civilisation on Mars.

HE   I'm not sure it was as bad as that, because already manned probes were forging further out into the system and the realm of the gas giants, mighty Jupiter, Saturn, Uranus and Neptune. Unexplained activity had been sighted between Neptune and its large satellite, Triton. So a base was established on Jupiter's moon, Ganymede—

SHE I have visited Ganymede City. It's a pretty swinging place. People live for the day. I fear Mars gets bypassed now, because views of Jupiter from Ganymede and the other moons are so inexhaustibly wonder-making.

HE   From Ganymede, it was just a hop to the neighbouring moon, Oceania – the rechristened Europa – where views of Jupiter are even more stunning.

There's a floating base on Oceania, built on top of a kilometre-deep ice floe. Under the ice crust, remarkably, is a fresh water ocean – pure fresh water, without life, or without life until we seeded some there.

That water gets despatched in bladdees to Mars. Mars now has a large lake slowly turning into a sea of fresh water. Its main problem is solved.

SHE   And so of course Mars is being terraformed, at last. The human race has moved on and no longer needs a monument to old dreams and illusions.

HE   Mars's period of frugal utopia did not last. But the blackness of the twentieth century, with all its wars, genocides, killings, injustice and greed had faded away. Somehow, we found the strength, in Bligh's words, to stay our hand. The human race is happier – less tormented – as it launches out towards the stars.

SHE   To meet with all those other species we don't yet know of . . . Maybe with God?

HE   Unlikely. God was one of those creaking floorboards in the brain we left behind when we got to Mars.

SHE   I cannot accept that. What would become of the human race if there was no god?

HE   What became of it during the twentieth century when supposedly there was a god? You believers might say, 'He saved us from destroying ourselves with our nuclear weapons. That was his will.' Equally, if we had destroyed ourselves, that would have been God's will too, according to you. There's no God – yet I hate him. I hate the way religious belief has caused us to waste our energies looking away from our own intractable problems. He stood in our way of enlightenment, like Jung's Shadow, barring us from accepting that we are made of the ashes fallen from the flanks of extinct suns. That we are universe-stuff. The universe is where we belong.

SHE   You must allow me strongly to disagree. God has been our inspiration, lifting us from the material. Have you never listened to all the beautiful sacred music composed in his name, or seen all the great paintings faith has inspired?

HE   The paintings were painted by men. God didn't have half the musical genius of Johann Sebastian Bach, I can tell you. You must give up this illusion, comforting although it is. Giving it up is part of the process of becoming adult.

SHE   I don't understand you.

HE   You mean you don't understand evolution.

SHE   Don't be silly. Science and religion are not in conflict.

HE   No – it's experience and religion which are in conflict.

SHE   And what will we do without God?

HE   We must learn – as we are slowly learning – to judge ourselves, and our own actions.

SHE   You won't shake my faith. I'm sorry you don't have it.

HE   Faith? Being unmoved by facts? Come, you must not pride yourself on such blindness. Think how the concept of God separated us from the rest of nature, set us above the animals, gave us the example of puissance and abasement. Made us self-preoccupied idiots.

SHE   That's blasphemous rubbish. You sound almost inhuman when you speak like that.

HE   We are almost becoming another species, we spacegoers. Physical and mental change is rapid now. We have developed from the gifts of that tormented

twentieth century, from the discovery of the DNA
code and the subsequent advance of genetic engineering. The bladdees shuttling to and fro across
matrix between Oceania and Mars are living entities
developed by bio-engineering skills from the modest
bladder-wort.

SHE   You remember the excitement when Ganymede was
made habitable by new plant-insect stock. The
plantsects were despatched in unmanned probes.
They soft-landed on Ganymede, dispersed, reproduced rapidly, and prepared the satellite for us when
we arrived there. By that time, the plantsects had cul-
minated, consuming themselves, leaving their bodies
for compost. Such advances would have been impossible in the early days of Mars landings, with their
mechanistic approach.

HE   And did God walk on Ganymede? No, he stood in
our way! Was he not Carl Jung's monstrous Shadow,
cutting ourselves off from a realisation of ourselves as
being intrinsically a part of the whole cosmos – ashes
from extinct suns?

SHE   Try to love God, whether or not you think he exists.
Hatred is harmful to you. God was necessary – essential, perhaps – for some ages past, and the Saviour
represented a condition for us to aspire to in the long
period of darkness.

HE   (Laughs) You're saying we have saved ourselves?

SHE   I'm saying only that the concept of a loving Saviour
helped us, once upon a time. But certainly we've
done away with hatred on the outer satellites, along
with most forms of illness; genetic revision and
improved immune systems have altogether clarified
our minds.

HE   It was the understanding that we are an intrinsic part
      of nature which transformed our perceptions when
      we arrived on Mars. Much has followed. The bleak
      Martian globe cleared our minds. A prompting of our
      symbiotic relationship with plant life speeded the
      development of warm-blooded plants. It has radically
      changed our being and appearance. That epiphyte
      growing on your head, much resembling an orchid, is
      now women's crowning glory! It permits you to carry
      with you a micro-atmosphere, a temperature-gauge
      and other perceptions, wherever you go.

SHE   As do the ferns sprouting round your venerable cra-
      nium. You are right there. We're now true terrestrials,
      half-human, half-plant, creatures of nature, well-
      equipped to venture throughout a waiting universe.

HE   Well, it's been pleasant to talk with you. You must go
      on your way. I have to retire; I'm growing too old to
      travel. We shall not meet again. Farewell, dear spirit!